P9-BZJ-972

"These spells of yours seem to be increasing, Dawna,"

the doctor told her.

"I'm Maurie Miller," she said frantically. "Maurie Miller."

"Stop that nonsense this minute," he ordered sharply. "I have to warn you that your husband is concerned about your behavior. Even your own child is afraid of you."

She's not my child—I don't have a child. The protest died in her throat. *The child is afraid of me because she alone recognizes that I'm not her mother.* "I'm Maurie Miller—I don't have a husband or a child. The girl is the only one who knows the truth!"

"And what is the truth, dear?" the doctor asked with polite impatience.

Maurie's voice trembled. "I'm caught in the web of a dream, a nightmare, and I can't wake up."

He just looked at her for a long moment, and then he opened his black medical bag. With an unhurried movement, he filled a syringe....

Dear Reader,

The nights are getting cooler now that fall is here, and that means it will be even easier for you to shiver as you read the wonderful new Shadows novels we've got for you.

In *Footsteps in the Night,* Lee Karr tells the story of a heroine whose trip to Ireland turns frightening as she keeps finding herself trapped inside another woman's body, another woman's life. No matter where she turns, danger seems to beckon, and the only man who can save her may be the one man she doesn't dare to trust.

Jane Toombs offers *What Waits Below,* a story of a family with dark and terrifying secrets, and a link to the past that may prove fatal—especially to the heroine. Only the mysterious new groundskeeper seems to have an idea what's going on, but even if he's on her side, will their united efforts be enough to save her from the tentacles of the family curse?

In months to come, we'll chill you even further with books by favorite writers, such as mainstream's Patricia Simpson, as well as the new authors we'll be bringing your way. So be sure to look for your reading pleasure in the shadows—Silhouette Shadows.

Yours,

Leslie Wainger
Senior Editor and Editorial Coordinator

LEE KARR

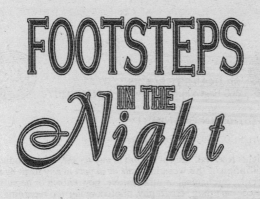

FOOTSTEPS IN THE Night

Published by Silhouette Books New York

America's Publisher of Contemporary Romance

If you purchased this book without a cover you should be aware that this book is stolen property. It was reported as "unsold and destroyed" to the publisher, and neither the author nor the publisher has received any payment for this "stripped book."

SILHOUETTE BOOKS
300 East 42nd St., New York, N.Y. 10017

FOOTSTEPS IN THE NIGHT

Copyright © 1993 by Leona Karr

All rights reserved. Except for use in any review, the reproduction or utilization of this work in whole or in part in any form by any electronic, mechanical or other means, now known or hereafter invented, including xerography, photocopying and recording, or in any information storage or retrieval system, is forbidden without the permission of the publisher, Silhouette Books, 300 E. 42nd St., New York, N.Y. 10017

ISBN: 0-373-27015-1

First Silhouette Books printing September 1993

All the characters in this book have no existence outside the imagination of the author and have no relation whatsoever to anyone bearing the same name or names. They are not even distantly inspired by any individual known or unknown to the author, and all incidents are pure invention.

® and ™:Trademarks used with authorization. Trademarks indicated with ® are registered in the United States Patent and Trademark Office, the Canada Trade Mark Office and in other countries.

Printed in the U.S.A.

Books by Lee Karr

Silhouette Shadows

Stranger in the Mist #3
Footsteps in the Night #15

LEE KARR

is a multipublished author of Gothic romances and suspense novels. An avid reader, her favorite books have always been those that send her heart pounding and bring a dry lump of fear to her throat. When she isn't writing and reading, she enjoys visiting her four children and traveling into the Colorado mountains with her husband, Marshall.

To Jasmine Cresswell,
whose friendship is a delight and a joy, always

CHAPTER ONE

An ominous rumbling of thunder accompanied clouds darkening the Irish countryside. Heavy rain still confined Maureen Miller to the small room she had rented in a boardinghouse just outside the tiny coastal village of Glenmara. She stood at the second-floor window looking out on a steep slate roof where masses of green black ivy clung to the stone exterior. Shiny wet leaves of the vine smothered the old farmhouse with a choking malignancy and put the room in shadow. Maurie's gaze followed the country landscape stretching away bleakly in the relentless drizzle. The brooding scene reminded her of Celtic tales filled with dark creatures who worked their evil magic in murky loughs and forests.

A sense of uneasiness settled upon her as she turned away from the window. Lying down on her narrow bed, she felt an insidious chill from the April rain. There had been nothing but rain since she had stepped off the plane at Shannon International two days ago. She drew a knitted coverlet over her as she thought about the preparations she'd made the past few weeks—her leave of absence from the small New

England college where she taught, subleting her apartment and successfully finding a tender, loving home for her cat, Buzzie.

On the edge of sleep, Maurie heard the landlady, Mrs. Duffy, talking in her rich Irish brogue to a new boarder, Mr. Daylan O'Shane, who had taken a room down the hall the day before. Their voices faded and were replaced by the hypnotic brush of rain on the roof.

I'm here, she thought before she fell asleep. *Tomorrow I'll begin the search for my Irish roots.*

She didn't know how long she'd been asleep when a strange awareness came over her. She could hear the rain peppering the window pane, but another sound pushed its way into her consciousness. A music box. A tinkling melody mingled with the sound of hushed voices. Must be the landlady and the new boarder outside her door...with a music box, she thought lazily, her eyes still closed. She pulled the coverlet up over her shoulders, but the familiar feel of knitted yarn had changed to a caressing softness. Her fingers slid over a soft down-filled quilt. With a start, she realized that her cheek was resting on a pillowcase as smooth as satin. She raised her head and stared at a satin pillowcase embroidered with the initials C.C. And suddenly she realized she was lying on the middle of a wide bed fashioned with a high headboard and four carved posts.

Slowly she sat up. *I'm dreaming,* she thought on some detached level. The tiny farmhouse bedroom had changed into an enormous bedchamber with richly paneled walls and a high ceiling ribbed with elaborate moldings. Mullioned glass windows spanned a wall framed by lovely swags of deep green draperies. Only a modern television console built into a wall facing her bed was at odds with the castlelike bedchamber.

I'm dreaming. Awake and yet still asleep. She hated that trapped feeling. Wanting to wake up and not being able to throw off the mantle of sleep. Her head felt heavy. She moved her arms as if they were weighted, and she couldn't see into the far corners of the room.

She lay back down, closing her eyes tightly. In a moment, she would awaken. The weird dream would be gone. She'd be back in the narrow bed in the room she'd rented with the smell of roasting meat and potatoes floating up from the kitchen below as Mrs. Duffy prepared supper for her four boarders. Yes, in a minute she would wake up, she told herself. Maybe she wouldn't even remember this dream. She'd never been one to clearly recall dreams. But why was this one so real?

She could still hear pattering rain ... and the music box. A lilting tune. She tried to place it. Irish? English? "Londonderry Air." That's what it was. She felt strangely satisfied that she had identified the song.

A childish giggle made her slowly turn her head toward two figures illumined by a circle of light cast by a small lamp as they sat on a chaise longue against one wall of the room. A gray-haired woman smiled down at a child sitting on her lap. The dark-haired little girl giggled as she watched a horse on a music box go round and round.

Maurie tried to speak. She wanted to say something—but she couldn't. *It's part of the dream. The horrible part of being awake and yet still asleep.* With concentrated effort, she threw back the silken quilt and slid her legs over the side of the bed until her bare feet brushed the soft fibers of a plush carpet. A rain-laden wind splashing against the windows brought a bone-deep chill to her body. Shivering, she hugged herself, startled to find she was wearing a long blue nightgown and matching bed jacket.

The woman looked up. "Oh, Mrs. Fitzgerald, you're awake, and a nice nap ye've been having, too. Feeling better, are ye? Hollie, dear, Mommy's awake." She carried the child over to the bed. "Give Mommy a kiss."

The frightened one-year-old clung to her nanny's neck desperately. She turned her head away and buried her face in the plump little woman's neck.

"'Tis just childish shyness, Mrs. Fitzgerald," apologized the woman. "Ye being sick and all. The little one doesn't understand that her mother—"

"No...I'm not...her mother," Maurie managed. Her voice sounded different.

"But of course ye are. It's ill you've been, and things are a wee bit mixed up for ye, that's all."

"I'm Maurie Miller. Maureen Miller."

"Go on with ye." The woman gave a nervous laugh. "Ye be Dawna Fitzgerald—Mrs. Oliver Fitzgerald, and mother of wee Hollie here."

"No...no, I'm not." *Why can't I wake up?* "I am not Mrs. Fitzgerald," she said defiantly. She tried to explain that this was all a dream, but a rush of incoherent words made her put her hands to her face. The British accent in her voice was unmistakable. What was happening? Where was her own American speech? Why was a stranger's voice coming out of her mouth? *It's a dream—only a dream,* she schooled herself as a trembling attacked her body. "I'm Maurie...Maurie..."

The little girl looked into Maurie's face, and as if she beheld a stranger in her mother's bed, she began to cry.

"Hush, hush, darlin'. Yer Mommy's just having a bad spell. We'll call the nurse. Miss Doughty will take care of her." The nanny flung an anxious look over her shoulder as she clutched the child and hurried out of the room.

Maurie got to her feet, weak and wavery. She walked around the bed to a light switch as if she had known exactly where it was located on the wall. She stood there in her bare feet and fancy nightclothes, letting her gaze travel around the room. The furnishings were a mixture of modern and period, all tastefully blended. Beautiful frescoes decorated the high ceiling, and a colorful French tapestry hung on the wall. Chairs and sofas were clustered in an inviting pattern in front of a marble fireplace. A highboy and chest of drawers matched the four-poster, and nearby, a dressing table was laden with numerous bottles, a jewelry box and a silver comb-and-brush set.

Maurie moved slowly over to the dressing table. With rounded eyes she looked at her reflection in the gilded mirror. The face was her own—and yet different. Thinner. *As if I've been ill.* The arched eyebrows had the same uplift over azure blue eyes, but she'd never worn her hair like this, long with soft waves flowing over her shoulders. As her fingers threaded the thick dark strands, she felt the roots pulling against her skull.

"Dawna, what are you doing out of bed? Look at you, standing there shivering. For heaven's sake! Don't you want to get well?" A young woman wearing a petal pink sweater over a white nurse's uniform scolded her impatiently. Her flaxed hair was primly held back with a stunning onyx barrette at the nape of her neck. "Now you get back in bed. It's time for your medicine."

"No...I..." stammered Maurie. "You don't understand...."

"No argument or I'll tell Oliver." The nurse's flinty blue eyes glinted with satisfaction. "And you know how short his temper is—especially when you insist on being difficult. I don't know why you make it so hard on yourself." Her rather pretty features could have been chipped out of ice. Hard mouth, thin nose and arrogant chin. "It's really very stupid of you, Dawna."

"I'm not Dawna." Maurie's voice quivered. When would the nightmare end? She was sick and frightened. She didn't want to be here—threatened by the nurse and somebody named Oliver. She wanted to wake up. She wanted her subconscious to swallow up the nightmare and never allow it to float to the surface again.

"You're not well," the nurse said with a hint of satisfaction. "No one would be surprised if your melancholy drove you to some unfortunate behavior, Dawna. Something dreadful could happen—any day."

"Leave me alone." Maurie could see the hateful derision in the young woman's smile.

"You really have no choice, you know. Surely you realize that by now. Oliver always wins—one way or another."

The ominous threat made Maurie shiver.

"You're cold," the nurse said flatly. "Get back in bed."

Maurie resisted the firm hand on her arm, but the slender woman was strong and propelled her back to the bed. Then she handed Maurie two small pills and a glass of water. "Take them, Dawna."

No...no, she protested silently, but seemed unable to resist. As if she was used to obeying that tone of voice, Maurie swallowed the pills.

"Good girl," said Miss Doughty in a falsely bright tone. "Are you cold, Dawna? I'll turn up the heat a bit. I don't think I'll ever get used to this miserable wet climate. We had rain in London, but it didn't have this bloody never-ending chill, day after day. The sun would come out and dry everything. Remember?"

"I've never been to London," said Maurie in that weird British voice that wasn't her own.

"Dawna!" The woman's light blue eyes were hard as stones. "I don't know what kind of game you're playing now, but Oliver won't be amused." The warning edge in her voice brought a tightening to Maurie's chest.

"I'm an American," Maurie protested in clipped British tones. "This is a horrible nightmare...."

"Your husband is running out of patience, Dawna. This new little subterfuge will only infuriate him even more." With that pronouncement she flounced out of the room and Maurie heard a key turning in the lock.

An urgency denied the dreamlike quality of Maurie's thoughts. She was in danger. A malevolent threat hung over her and some horror seemed ready to pounce on her. *I'm not Dawna...I'm not Dawna.* The silent cry brought Maurie to her feet, and she stumbled over to one of the arched mullioned windows.

Through gray sheets of rain, she glimpsed the ground far below. No boardinghouse slate roof with grasping ivy met her eyes, no familiar yard nor kitchen garden. Nothing familiar. The murky view was of dark drifts of trees and crazed white surf far below beating against high cliffs. Where was she? Why was she dreaming of danger? Why was fear creeping up the middle of her back like something alive? She looked up and saw an openmouthed gargoyle staring down at her from a high ledge, rain pouring out of its mouth.

She jerked back. Terror like the crest of a wave washed over her. There had to be a way out of the nightmare. *Where am I? Why can't I wake up?*

A half-opened door at one end of the room caught her eye, and she hurried toward it. Once again her fingers seemed to find the light switch just inside the bathroom familiar. *As if I've been here before!* Impossible. There was nothing familiar about the luxurious peach carpet covering the bathroom floor nor the decorative tiles lining the walls and a glass-enclosed shower stall. Modern ivory fixtures and beautiful arched windows were like those pictured in millionaires' homes.

Maurie's head began to ache and her limbs felt light, as if the pills were beginning to take effect. She saw a closed door at the far end of the spacious bathroom. The shining brass doorknob felt cold as she clasped it slowly. Cautiously she let the door swing all the way open before she stepped into an adjoining bedroom.

A man stood with his back to her. He held a cigarette in one hand and a sheaf of papers in the other. A brocade smoking jacket stretched across his broad shoulders. She must have made some sound, for he swung around and his expression instantly hardened. A flash of cold impatience flickered in his deep-set, piercing brown-black eyes. He had black hair that waved back from a high forehead and a precisely trimmed mustache that added to the rigidity of unsmiling lips. "What are you doing out of bed, Dawna?"

This must be Oliver, Maurie thought on some detached level. Once more she tried to explain that she was caught in a nightmare. "This isn't real. I'll wake up. I'm not Dawna."

"Stop it. I won't have my wife talking gibberish," he said and clenched his fists.

"You have to believe me. My name is Maureen Miller and I don't talk like this. I'm not English. I'm American."

"That does it, Dawna. My patience has run out." His glare was contemptuous. He threw down the papers and stamped out his cigarette. "You're no good to anyone the way you are. I'm going to call the doctor. There's a sanitarium—"

"Listen to me!" Panic swelled up and choked her. "I'm a college instructor from the States. Twenty-nine years old, and I'm not married. *You* are not my husband. I don't have a child." In a trembling voice,

Maurie heard herself explaining that she'd been born in Ireland and taken to America by her adoptive parents. She watched the man's face as she told him how she'd decided to take a year's leave of absence to find out whatever she could about her Irish heritage. "So you see, I'm not Dawna.... I don't know why I'm dreaming this."

His face flared with anger. "You like to torment me, don't you? Delight in thwarting me at every turn. I'm warning you, I've had enough of your stupid stubbornness."

As he took a threatening step toward her, Maurie backed up. Frightened, she spun around to flee and lost her balance. She went down on one knee. Her cheek hit the edge of the open door. She screamed loudly.

Her arms flailed the knitted coverlet that lay over her. A pounding on her door vibrated through the small bedroom and brought her straight up in the small bed.

"Open the door!"

Hot sweat beaded on her brow and her body was trembling. She was in her small rented room again. Someone was in the hall calling to her and knocking on the door. She staggered to her feet. Crossed the room. With shaking hands, she slipped the simple bolt. The door opened and the new boarder, Daylan O'Shane, stood there. "What's wrong, Maurie? I heard you screaming."

His hair was the same raven black as the threatening Oliver's. Arched eyebrows shadowed his dark eyes, and in a terrifying moment his face and the one in her dream mingled. Panic stricken, she tried to shut the door. Maybe she wasn't awake, after all—just dreaming she was back in her room. *Wake up... wake up.*

He blocked the doorway with one of his legs.

"No...no," she choked, trying to force the door closed. The nightmare was still upon her. Fright quivered in her chest. Her skin prickled with danger.

"It's all right. I only want to help. What's frightening you, Maurie?"

She croaked, "You're Oliver."

He raised a black eyebrow. "Oliver? Who's Oliver? You're confused, Maurie. Don't you remember? We met yesterday when I moved in? Daylan O'Shane?"

His voice was different. Softer and yet deeper, filled with a soothing patience. Not like the man in her dream who lashed out at her with threats.

"I assure you, Maurie, I didn't mean to startle you. I was going past your room...heard you screaming."

She put a hand to her forehead. It was moist with cold beads of perspiration.

He touched her arm gently. "What is it, Maurie?"

"I...I..." she stammered. "I don't know how to explain."

"Try."

She looked up at him and realized then that he had called her Maurie, not Dawna. She was awake now. Fully awake. She was standing in the doorway of her room. The smell of roasting meat floated up from the kitchen downstairs. She gave a sob of relief.

"All right now?" His hand smoothed back a moist brown curl drifting forward on her cheek.

She nodded. "I was napping and . . . and had a bad dream." How simple it sounded. A nightmare. A child's terror. Nothing more. She was embarrassed that she had reacted so violently. "It was a strange dream."

"It must have been. From the way you were screaming, I expected to find a room full of banshees." He grinned in a reassuring way. "My grandmother used to say those ghostly phantoms loved to come out in the rain, wailing and moaning to keep death away."

She shivered. Death. Was Dawna going to die? She suppressed the idiotic question. Nobody really died in a dream, did they? And that's all it was. A trick of her subconscious. The nightmare would fade. She was surprised by how vividly she remembered it.

"You still look a little pale," he said. He touched her face again with a gentle fingertip. "There's a red spot on your cheek. Looks like you hit your face on something."

She must have wavered, for he reached out and steadied her. "What is it, Maurie?"

"The door. I hit my cheek on the door when I fell."

In my dream.

CHAPTER TWO

Maurie put a hand up to her cheek. The sensation of falling came back. Hitting her face on the edge of the door. No! That was only a dream. It couldn't have happened that way. She must have struck herself when she was flailing around in the bed trying to wake up. Yes, that's what happened.

Daylan's dark eyes narrowed as he watched the fleeting expressions on her face. "It's just a tiny red spot," he assured her. "Nothing to worry about."

She managed a tremulous smile. *Nothing to worry about.* She took herself in hand. "You're right. I'm sorry. You must think I'm a ninny to be acting this way because of a nightmare." *But it was so real.*

"What you need is a cup of strong tea—just the kind Mrs. Duffy makes. My nose tells me that she's about to put supper on the table." He sniffed the air pointedly. "A lamb stew if I don't miss my guess. Care to make a bet?"

Responding to his engaging smile, she countered, "Smells more like roast beef."

"It's a wager. Loser has to buy a round of drinks at the village pub after supper." There was a challenge, as well as an invitation, in his dark eyes.

"Is this a subtle Irish way of getting a date by any chance?" she parried.

"Not subtle enough, I guess," he admitted with a grin that did nice things to his face. "You American women are pretty perceptive."

She felt the weight of the bad dream lifting from her shoulders. She smiled back. "And a sucker for a smooth line. Let me freshen up and I'll join you downstairs."

"Great."

She watched him saunter down the hall and for a moment her heart tightened. The muscular lines of his shoulders, the breadth of his back and the tufts of raven hair curling down the nape of his neck were startlingly familiar. *Like Oliver before he turned around.* Then she mentally shook herself. No. It wasn't the same man at all. The color of his hair was the only thing that really matched—and she'd seen plenty of Irishmen with that same jet black hair.

She quickly closed the door and leaned up against it, listening to his footsteps descending the stairs. In spite of herself, a deep disquiet lingered. As her gaze passed over the narrow bed, she clearly remembered the mammoth four-poster of her dream, the firmness of the mattress and the feel of the satin pillowcases with the embroidered monogram. She looked at the square window dark with rain and fog, and an imprint of arched mullioned windows lingered in her mind's eye.

Slowly she walked across the room until she stood in front of the modest mirror hanging above a low rustic dresser. Like someone mesmerized, she stared at her reflection with wide, azure blue eyes. Her short feathered curls were the same burnished dark brown as the long strands she had seen drifting around her face in the gilded mirror of the lady's dressing table. The eyes, nose and mouth were similar and yet different. A healthy roundness in the lines and planes of her own face was at odds with the face she'd seen in her nightmare. *But Dawna had been ill.*

Maurie reached up and touched the mark on her cheek. The redness was fading. Soon it would be gone—like the memory of her dream. And all the people her imagination had created would sink into her subconscious and be forgotten.

She gave a shaky laugh. Irish literature was filled with tales of superstitions and supernatural creatures who wrought their revenge upon foolish mortals. Obviously she'd been too eager to claim her cultural heritage by reading absorbing stories of ghosts, demons, leprechauns, banshees and fanciful wee folk. The dark beauty of the Emerald Isle must be responsible for the weird creations of such myths, Maurie decided as she listened to the rain and tried to dispel an invading foreboding that defied all logic.

She changed into a soft blue sweater and matching stretch pants. A paisley scarf tied casually around her neck brought out the blue of her eyes. She wore only a touch of blush on her cheeks and a faint pink lipstick on her mouth. Most of the time she was taken for a student, instead of a professor, at the small college where she taught. At twenty-nine, she was the youngest member on the staff.

Wonderful aromas were floating out of the kitchen as she went downstairs. The landlady fed her boarders well, and Maurie knew she'd have to resist some of the good Irish cooking or gain twenty pounds before she returned home.

She poked her head through the kitchen doorway. The plump, squarely built Irish woman was bent over, taking a tray of freshly baked rolls out of a mammoth oven.

"Can I give you a hand, Mrs. Duffy?"

The landlady's round face was flushed from the heat of a stove fired hotly with turf. Strands of wiry sandy hair had slipped away from a knotted twist on the top of her head, and her face glistened with sweat. She handled the hot pan with the finesse of a juggler, and after she studied each browned bun, the satisfied expression of an artist crossed her face. "There's been a bit of a waiting on these, but they're done now."

"Smells wonderful," Maurie said as the aroma of hot bread teased her nostrils. "My mother used to bake before she became ill. I'd come home for school, and the smell of freshly baked bread would greet me. She'd cut me a big slice and load it down with butter and strawberry jelly.''

''Nothing better,'' Mrs. Duffy agreed.

A movement on the other side of the stove made her realize that Mrs. Duffy wasn't alone in the kitchen. Maurie was startled to see a wizened little woman sitting in one of the kitchen chairs beside the huge cook stove.

Maurie nodded in recognition and the woman nodded back. Her face was brown and wrinkled, and her eyes were as black as coal. She wore a pair of faded men's trousers, a shapeless knit sweater that drooped over her slight frame and a faded scarf tied Gypsy-style around her graying head. A spray of tiny yellow button flowers was pinned like a corsage on one thin shoulder. Muddy boots and socks lay in a tumbled heap beside the chair. The woman continued to hold out bluish bare feet toward the warmth of the stove as her bright black eyes traveled over Maurie's face.

''Maureen Miller, be ye,'' the woman said in a tone that indicated no confirmation was needed. Her voice was full and strong, incongruous with the impression of physical fragility. ''Fresh from Amer-i-ca.''

Maurie nodded. Mrs. Duffy must keep her friends fully informed about her boarders, she thought. ''Yes, I arrived a couple of days ago.''

''So I hear.''

Undoubtedly the small village had a well-oiled gossip pipeline, Maurie mused, glad she hadn't talked to anyone about her real reason for coming to Glenmara. She'd always treasured her privacy and had told Mrs. Duffy that she was in Ireland to do independent research for an academic publication. She'd kept her personal reason for coming to her birthplace to herself, not telling anyone she'd been born in Ireland and brought as an infant to America by adoptive parents.

Something akin to amusement chased across the wizened woman's face, as if she'd read Maurie's thoughts. "Come back to dig for your roots, have ye?"

Maurie stared at her. *How did she know?*

"'Tis an Irish name, she has, for sure," offered Mrs. Duffy as she continued to bustle about preparing the evening meal.

Of course, that was it. The name "Maureen" hinted at Irish blood. The woman must be a local character, thought Maurie, trying to dismiss those black dagger eyes that pinned her with their sharpness. There was no reason to feel she was being stripped bare by the weird little woman's unblinking gaze.

"What's your name?" Maurie asked politely.

"Tansie."

Maurie's eyes went to the spray of yellow flowers pinned on the woman's shapeless sweater. Before she could say anything, the woman's tiny hands whipped off the spray of flowers and held it out to her. "Have a bit of tansy."

The flowers had a strong unpleasant smell, and Maurie's nose quivered as she shook her head. "Thank you but—"

"You'll be needing them—for your bad dreams and all."

Maurie's mouth went dry. "What do you mean— bad dreams?" The odor of the tansy flowers filled Maurie's nostrils. An icy coil of fear twisted her insides. "What do you mean?" she repeated.

Tansie gave Maurie a knowing smile as she fingered the sprig in her hands. Then a dark cloud passed over her eyes as she said in a solemn tone, "Beware of losing your way in a web of dreams."

Maurie couldn't find her voice. The air was charged with an ominous stillness.

"Dear, would you mind filling the bowls I set out on the dining room table?" Mrs. Duffy asked Maurie, breaking the silence. She handed Maurie a steaming tureen and ladle. "That's a good girl. I'll bring in the other dishes."

Maurie avoided looking in the direction of the hypnotic little woman, and once in the dining room, she began to breathe easier. Probably everyone visiting Ireland had dreams of one sort or another, Maurie reasoned. Heaven only knew the brooding atmosphere was enough to cause all kinds of nightmares. No doubt Tansie was a harmless eccentric with a gift for the dramatic.

Five places had been set at the table, four for boarders and one for Mrs. Duffy. In addition to Maurie and Daylan, there were two more guests, a middle-aged English couple who were on a month's holiday in the area. The outgoing Mr. and Mrs. Morehead had been quite sociable and kept previous table conversation lively, talking about historical sights to be seen in the area.

Maurie finished filling the bowls. Lamb stew—so Daylan had guessed right. She suspected he'd been snooping around the kitchen earlier and the wager had just been a clever way to ask her out. She'd have to watch out for his smooth charm. Daylan O'Shane was the most attractive man she'd encountered in a long time. She let out a deep breath. Ireland certainly seemed to be a place of heightened emotions.

When Maurie took the empty tureen back into the kitchen, Tansie was sitting at the table, still barefoot, and the witchlike little woman didn't look up from her generous helping of stew and bread as Maurie passed.

"Come along, dear," Mrs. Duffy said to Maurie. "We're ready now."

Mr. and Mrs. Morehead, who had been waiting in the sitting room, responded to the dinner bell. As Daylan came into the dining room, he took a pipe out of his mouth. She didn't know why she was glad to know he smoked a pipe. Then she remembered. *Oliver had been smoking a cigarette.* He held out her chair in a gentlemanly gesture before taking one across the table from her. She was poignantly aware of his presence and was glad when the English couple engaged him in conversation. They asked him if he was familiar with the Cliffs of Moher, a famous attraction on the western coast.

"A spectacular sight," Mrs. Morehead declared. "Gave me the shivers the way the wind blew across the top of the cliffs, and the drop to the ground was sheer and hundreds of feet below. The caretaker at O'Brians tower said that the cliffs were haunted."

Her husband snorted.

Daylan leaned across the table toward her. "You must be referring to the Dread Women of Moher who fly over the cliffs in stormy weather looking for a bloody banquet," he said solemnly.

Mrs. Morehead's eyes widened. "Really? How... grim."

Daylan's brogue deepened. "I know the cliffs well, sure and haunted they be. A storm came sweeping in from the Atlantic when I was just a lad, catching me a mile from the cottage my parents had rented for a holiday. Black clouds mounted high, lightning sliced the sky, and winged monsters rose from the angry white sprays climbing the cliffs below me. I saw them with me own eyes, I did. A horrible rumble from the sea warned me that the Dread Women of Moher were after me. Sure and the furies of hell were at my heels as I ran for the shelter of my house before they caught me." He lowered his voice in a prophetic whisper. "Some say these women, these harbingers of disaster, are among us—in disguise."

Mrs. Morehead gave a nervous titter. Her husband looked amused. Maurie lowered her eyes, hoping no one would sense the sudden quickening of her heartbeat. She knew that Daylan was just spinning a ghost story, but the bizarre old woman sitting in the kitchen lent a bone-chilling reality to the tale. And the dark intensity of Daylan's expression made him seem strange and unfamiliar. Maurie was glad when the conversation moved on to a variety of mundane topics, including the weather.

"Begorra, if you see dark clouds on the horizon," Mrs. Duffy told them, "you know it's going to rain. If you don't see any clouds, you know it *is* raining."

"We're used to rain in London," declared perky Mrs. Morehead. "But the sun warms up everything quickly once it decides to shine."

The piece of bread in Maurie's mouth was suddenly dry. *The nurse in her dream. She'd said something like that.* The memory was still crystal clear—not like most nightmares. Maurie could still remember what the people looked like and what they'd said. She closed her eyes for a moment, and when she opened them she saw that Daylan was watching her from across the table.

A speculating glint in his eyes matched a slight furrowing of his forehead. "Maurie?"

Good heavens, what must he be thinking? A warm flush crept up her neck. She firmed her chin and smiled. "Delicious lamb stew."

"My nose never lets me down," he quipped with a teasing grin.

"Nor your eyes, either?" she challenged.

"Are you suggesting skullduggery on my part, Miss Miller?" He put a hand on his chest as if pained.

She leaned toward him and asked as solemnly as a judge, "Were you in the kitchen before dinner?"

Mrs. Duffy answered for him. "Aye, the lad was kind enough to bring in vegetables from the dirt cellar. Even helped me peel the taters. He was a tellin' me about his grandmother's Irish stew. And how is the dish comparing with your grandmother's recipe?"

"She's met her match," he said gallantly. "And never did she equal the rich texture of these rolls. And the butter—I'm guessing it came from your very own churn." His brogue was suddenly quite heavy. He seemed able to turn it on and off as the moment dictated.

The landlady beamed under his flattery, and Mrs. Morehead touched his arm to coax his handsome raven head in her direction. "And where in Ireland is home, Mr. O'Shane?"

"Dublin. My grandmother still lives there in the family home—when she isn't traveling abroad. My parents live in London. They moved there several years ago when I was taking an advanced degree at Oxford." Now his inflection was slightly British.

"And what brings you to Glenmara?" Maurie asked.

"I'm a peddler," he answered smoothly.

"A peddler?" she echoed.

"Is there something wrong with such a time-honored profession?" he challenged.

"No, of course not," she said quickly. "But a graduate of Oxford..." she stammered, and then she recovered herself. "I'm sorry. I didn't mean to be rude. I hate it when someone insists that I fit into the stereotype of college professor."

"What do you teach?" he asked, deftly turning the conversation away from himself. Then he held up his hand. "Let me guess." He thought a moment. "English literature."

"What makes you think that?"

"There's something of the romantic about you. I'd guess you're a Byron and Browning scholar."

"You'd guess wrong. I teach pre-law courses."

"That would have been my second guess," he said quickly and everybody laughed, but there was a glint of wariness in his eyes that hadn't been there before. She felt his measuring eyes on her during the rest of the meal.

After coffee in the small sitting room, he approached her chair and gave a small bow. "Professor, shall we make our way through sleet and fog to Glenmara's merry public house?''

"I refuse to honor our bet," she answered with mock indignation. "You cheated."

"Guilty as charged." He reached for her hand. "Come on. The first tankard of Guinness is on me." He pulled her to her feet.

"But the weather . . ."

His brown eyes were like warm glowing embers as they settled on her face. "And what's wrong with a soft Irish rain kissing your cheeks? And the warmth of a friendly arm around your waist?" The timbre of his voice was like a caress.

Any feminine heart, young or old, would have to be cast in iron, Maurie thought, not to respond to his practiced charm. Any reservations she had about braving the miserable weather were changed by his smile.

An undefinable spiral of excitement put a lilt in her own voice. "I'll get my raincoat."

He drove a small British car that splashed through muddy puddles and sent water flying in the air like a rooster's tail.

"Nice car," she commented, noting that it was a late model equipped with all the accessories. She eyed the fashionable cut of his clothes.

"What do you . . . peddle?"

"Various things," he said vaguely in a tone that shut off more questions.

The Duffy farm was located a couple of miles east of town on a narrow country road, and they didn't pass any other cars until they reached the outskirts of the village. Glenmara's main street consisted of a long line of buildings facing a jagged coastline. Most of the business establishments were closed, but bright yellow light poured out of Kelly's Place, which dominated the main corner of the town.

Maurie could hear the swells of the Atlantic rising and falling in crashing rhythm, but land and sea were lost in thickened sheets of falling rain and a murky mist floating inland. The air was scented with odors of salt, kelp and seaweed.

Daylan parked in front of the tavern. They bounded out of the car and made a mad dash to the front door. Once inside, Maurie wasn't sure the place could hold two more customers. Smoke, moist air, body heat and strong ale filled her nostrils. Drinkers stood three deep at the bar, every small table was circled by more people than could fit around it and booths along the walls were crammed with merry drinkers. At the far end of the long room, a half-dozen musicians looking more like volunteers than professionals were playing fiddles and guitars. A small dance floor was filled with energetic couples stomping about while enthusiastic singers in the audience bellowed the lyrics of a popular folk song. Maurie's ears rang from a cacophony of voices, music and laughter. She was certain that walls and rafters were vibrating from the noise.

Daylan kept a firm grasp on her arm as they threaded their way through the crowd. A narrow staircase clung to one rough wall, and Daylan guided her up the wooden stairs to a small balcony. Several long tables and benches were crowded with people and Maurie didn't see anyplace to sit, but when Daylan paused at the end of one of the benches, everyone obligingly scooted over and he eased Maurie down beside him on the bench. Then he held up two fingers to a brawny waitress collecting empty mugs. She nodded as she swung the tray up one arm and then disappeared down another steep staircase leading to the bar.

"I hope you like Guinness," he said into her ear. "It's the best thing to order when the place gets crowded like this."

She nodded. "That'll be fine." She'd been wanting to taste the favorite drink of the Irish. Besides, she hardly needed alcohol to get into a party mood in this crowd. The contrast between the cold dank weather and the high-spirited friendly villagers was unbelievable. She could understand why taverns were community gathering places. The wave of hilarity was irresistible. She didn't understand half of what the people at her table were saying, but their rosy-cheeked smiles made her one of them.

She had a good view of the drinkers, singers and musicians on the main floor below. A pretty red-headed girl dressed in a skimpy green satin costume mingled with the crowd, selling cigarettes. After a few minutes she climbed the steps to the balcony and offered her tray of wares to Daylan. Standing provocatively on one foot with a nicely rounded hip touching him, she gave him a saucy wink and asked him how many packages he wanted.

He grinned at her, shook his head, took out a black pipe and stuck it unlit in his mouth. Maurie guessed from their banter that his smoking a pipe provided an ongoing dialogue between them. She wondered how well they knew each other, and her smile became forced. She was glad when the sexy girl moved on.

The drinks arrived and Maurie did her best to enjoy the strong brown ale, but she feared that Guinness was an acquired taste. Sipping her drink, she glanced over the railing and froze with the mug halfway to her mouth. A woman stood in the crowd below, looking around. Her flaxen hair was pulled back by an onyx barrette, and the lift of her chin and the chiseled hardness of her features brought instant recognition.

Maurie gasped. She set down the mug with such force that liquid spilled on the table. Then she lurched to her feet.

Daylan grabbed her arm. "What is it?"

"She's here."

"Who?"

Maurie jerked away. There wasn't time to explain. The woman was disappearing into the crowd. By the time Maurie had reached the lower level, the woman was almost at the front door. Maurie battled a swarm of merry customers as she frantically pushed her way through the crowd. "Please . . . please . . . let me by."

Several friendly souls laughingly slowed her progress, grabbing her arm and offering to buy her a drink as she tried to dodge past them. She heard Daylan behind her calling her name, but she didn't stop.

When she finally reached the front door, it was blocked by a burly policeman who was just coming in. He took a look at her anxious face. "Something the matter, miss?"

"No . . . nothing, thank you."

"You're sure?"

"Yes . . . I . . . I was just trying to catch someone." She gave him a fleeting smile as she pushed by him and dashed out onto the sidewalk. Rain poured off her head, and she swiped at her eyes so she could see through the deluge.

Watery light from the tavern windows shone out onto the sidewalks. She looked in both directions.

Empty.

The woman had disappeared.

"Maurie, what in heaven's name . . . ?" Daylan threw her raincoat over her shoulders and opened an umbrella over her head. Without waiting for an explanation he guided her to the car. Once inside, he started the engine and turned the heater on High.

She shivered uncontrollably and her teeth chattered. Her drenched hair dripped water onto her cheeks. He pulled her close and she pressed her wet face against the warmth of his chest. In the warm cocoon of his embrace, the turmoil inside her began to settle. She closed her eyes, wanting to shut out everything but this moment of peace—and sanity.

"What was that all about?" he asked evenly when her shudders had lessened.

For a moment she searched her mind for a lie, some believable explanation, but none came. In the end, she settled for the truth.

She straightened. "I saw her—Miss Doughty."

"Miss Doughty?"

"The nurse. The horrible woman in my dream."

CHAPTER THREE

Maurie couldn't see Daylan's expression clearly as they sat in the shadowy front seat, but the forced patience in his voice was clear. "You mean you rushed out of the pub after a woman who resembled someone in a dream?"

"Not *resembled*," Maurie flared. "It was her—the nurse! The same flaxen hair. Black onyx barrette. Same features and build. It was Miss Doughty."

For a moment he just sat there. Then he smoothed back a strand of drenched hair from her forehead. "Are you talking about the same dream you had this afternoon?"

"Yes...and that woman was in it." Her voice quivered. "How could that be?"

"Don't be getting yourself all worked up." He slipped an arm around her shoulder again and she could feel the warmth of his body through her damp clothing.

"But I recognized her."

"No great mystery," he reassured her quietly. "You've seen the gal someplace, somewhere and—"

"No, I haven't. Only in that awful dream."

"You may not consciously remember her," he insisted quietly. "But your mind kept a memory of the woman and produced her in your dream."

"No." Maurie set her jaw. "I'd never seen her before... before she showed up in my dream."

"Are you always this stubborn? Listen to me. Maybe she was a clerk at the airport, or a passenger who was on the same flight from New York, or you saw her waiting in the terminal. At the time, you might have only given her a fleeting glance, but something about the woman made an impression on you. Maybe the color of her hair or the way she moved."

Maurie searched her memory. Could he be right? "Do you think that's what happened?"

"I do, indeed."

There was such conviction in his tone that to argue further would appear juvenile and stubborn. Besides, what he said was logical and reassuring. More than anything she wanted to believe him. Why couldn't she shed the eerie disbelief that lingered in the shadows of her mind and accept his rational explanation? She could have seen the woman somewhere since her arrival in Ireland and for one reason or another had dreamed about her. But where had she seen her? When?

"What was she wearing in your dream?" he coaxed.

"A nurse's uniform... and pink sweater."

"And tonight?"

"Tan raincoat and pink scarf."

"And the first time you saw her, what was she wearing?"

It was a trick question and Maurie knew it. She waited for some mental picture to flash before her eyes—the way a name or fact could come to the surface when mentally searched for.

"What was the woman wearing when you first saw her?" Daylan repeated.

After a long moment she forced a laugh. "Nice try, but I drew a blank."

"It's all right. You'll remember sometime—when you're not trying."

"Yes...of course." She leaned her head back in the cradle of his arm and suppressed a bone-deep shiver.

"Are you always so intense about dreams and such?"

"No, not at all. I've always been very much a left-brain person. I've been accused of being terribly pragmatic, orderly and quite in touch with hard realities. I've never been guilty of emotional fantasies."

Until now. She'd been brought up with the Puritan work ethic, and her life had always been very stable, if not slightly dull. Her father had been a lawyer and her mother a staunch worker in the Protestant faith. All through school, she had studied hard, never giving in to impulsive acts, and all her romantic interludes had been the kind that kept both feet on the ground, causing only minor ripples in her life when they were over. "In fact, I rarely dream," she said aloud.

"But when you do, you have a pip, do you?" he chided. "It must be Ireland's dark magic at work."

"Nonsense," she retorted, but she had felt off balance ever since her arrival on Ireland's soil. Displaced. She'd been eagerly planning this trip ever since her parents had passed away within three years of each other, her mother from a blood disease and her father from thirty years of hard smoking. Coming to Ireland was the first decision she'd ever made that had been based on an emotional need she didn't quite understand. "Maybe I shouldn't have come," she murmured.

His fingertip lightly stroked her moist cheek. "You aren't going to let one haunting dream spoil your visit to the Emerald Isle, are you?"

Common sense demanded a sensible answer. "No, of course not." She gave a self-mocking laugh. In truth, now that the incident was over, she was truly embarrassed. "I am sorry I ran out like that," she said. "I really was enjoying myself."

"Good." He flashed her a smile.

She waited for him to say something about going to Kelly's again—but he didn't. Not that she could blame him. Twice today she'd behaved in a completely irrational manner—trying to slam the bedroom door on him and this last fiasco, rushing out of the pub like a crazed woman.

"We'd better head back so you can get into some warm, dry clothes." He gave her shoulder a light squeeze before he removed his arm.

Visibility was poor, but he drove the small car with practiced ease as the windshield wipers fought a losing battle with rivulets pouring down the glass. Watching his firm hands on the gearshift and the steering wheel, she was aware of a tensile strength that was at odds with the affable, low-key personality he projected.

Damp raven hair lay on his forehead, curling slightly from the rain. The balanced lines and planes of his face hinted at . . . a guarded control? She sensed that under his affable demeanor lay emotions ready to explode. He had a mouth that smiled easily, but his eyes always retained a certain glint, as if his mind was functioning on myriad levels. Even when he seemed to be giving her all his attention, she was conscious of a detachment that kept him aloof from the demands of the moment.

"The noise level in the pub was a little loud for talk," she said, giving in to a need to know more about him.

His mouth softened. "Talk?"

"I was all primed to inundate you with questions. From what was said at dinner tonight, you have an interesting family background. Your grandmother's in Dublin, your parents are in England, and you're here."

"Sounds as if we all need a lot of distance between us, doesn't it?" he answered. The smile faded as he kept his eyes focused on the road ahead.

"Do you need a lot of distance from your family?" she pried boldly.

He shot her a quick glance and then turned back to the road. "Actually my parents and I have always been very close," he answered evenly.

"And you're an only child?"

A muscle flickered in his cheek. "I am now." His hands tightened on the wheel. His voice grew gruff. "My younger sister was killed two years ago by a car bomb in Dublin, a block from our family home."

"Oh, I'm so sorry." Maurie silently chastised herself for bringing up the painful subject. She was well aware of the conflict in Northern Ireland, but it had been a distant happening until that moment, just something she had read about in the newspapers or seen on TV. Now, the sorrow in his voice and the pain in his face made it real and immediate. She was at a loss as to what to say.

"The innocent are always the ones who suffer," he added grimly. "You were wise to choose County Clare for your visit. Ulster has become a living hell, fueled by murder and more murder."

"Do you see any hope?"

"There's always hope," he said without any of it in his voice.

They fell silent and when he spoke again, his controlled easygoing demeanor was back in place. "What kind of study are you here about, Maurie?"

She could have given a vague answer, talked glibly about independent research, but the mood was one that invited confidence. He had shown his pain to her. She felt compelled to do the same. "Actually I'm here on a personal quest."

"What kind of quest?"

"I was born in Ireland, adopted by an American couple when I was an infant and raised in Philadelphia, Pennsylvania. I only legalized my United States citizen status when it came time for me to vote."

One of his dark eyebrows raised in surprise. "So, you're an Irish colleen, after all. And a name to match your heritage. Maureen." He said it softly. "Maureen."

She'd never had anyone speak her name like that. He endowed it with a lyrical quality that sent a tingling through her, as if the blood that flowed in her veins was suddenly endowed with the mysticism of emerald shamrocks, hidden loughs, craggy cliffs and the generations of Celtic people who had lived on this brooding island.

He frowned. "But Miller is wrong." He sent her a quick glance. "Do you have any idea . . . ?"

"Who my biological parents were?" she finished for him.

"Yes. You should have a name like Malone. Maureen Malone. That has a nice rhythm to it."

"How about Maureen O'Mallory?"

He looked startled. "Are you telling me you know your birth name?"

"Just my mother's name. With luck, I hope to find out a great deal more about her. I came across an old letter written to my adoptive parents by an Irish Catholic priest laying out the expenses that would have to be met before the final adoption papers were signed. In that letter a Father Flynn referred to my birth mother as Maelene O'Mallory."

"Maelene O'Mallory," he echoed. She was certain she felt him stiffen.

"Do you recognize the name?"

"Common name, O'Mallory," he said smoothly. His jaw worked as if he were about to say something more, but he held back any further comment.

"Do you have any suggestions how I should go about finding out what I want to know?"

"If you're determined to pursue the matter..."

"Of course. Why shouldn't I?"

"Sometimes it's better to leave the past behind."

Was there a warning in his tone? She studied his profile. His jaw had tightened and a frown deepened the furrows at the bridge of his nose. She felt subtle vibrations that defied interpretation. Then she shrugged. Must be her imagination.

"Didn't someone say that to know the past is to know the future?" she countered.

"I hope he was speaking of historical events and not people," Daylan answered shortly. "But it should be fairly easy to get the information you want. Church records are usually very reliable."

"You're Catholic?"

He nodded. "And you?"

"Raised Protestant."

"Well, if I can be of help, let me know. A bevy of Catholic sisters tried to civilize me when I was growing up. They predicted the devil would claim me as his own if I didn't mend my ways."

"And did you? Mend your ways?"

He gave her a roguish smile. "What do you think?"

"I don't know," she said honestly. Was it dangerous to take his teasing casual charm at face value? And perhaps even more dangerous to respond to the nebulous lightning beginning to arch between them? As she sat close to him in the seat and his long legs brushed against hers, the chill of the night was dispelled.

He pushed the button on a tape deck mounted under the dash, and the melodious tones of an Irish tenor drowned out the patter of rain on the roof and the splash of water under the wheels. The plaintive love song created a mood that was almost as unreal as her dream. She barely knew the man sitting beside her, and yet she was physically drawn to him, her emotions engaged on some mesmerizing level. Usually she was quite in control of her feelings when it came to men.

Strange. When she'd opened the bedroom door to him that afternoon, she'd been panic stricken by his resemblance to the horrible Oliver of her dream. Then she'd realized it was only the hair color and his general build that had given her that impression. Daylan said her subconscious had placed the flaxen-haired woman in her dream because she'd seen her somewhere. Was the same true of the resemblance Daylan had to Oliver? During his arrival at Mrs. Duffy's the day before, Daylan had seemed quite personable. Why would her subconscious cast him in such a frightening role? *Stop thinking about the nightmare!* she ordered herself, unable to control a shiver.

"Are you still cold?" he asked.

"A little," she lied. She wasn't going to mention the dream again. Daylan was an attractive man who had put up with a great deal of hysterics from her. She'd be lucky if he chose her company again.

She was startled when he boldly put one arm around her shoulders and drove with one hand.

"Is it safe?" she asked.

"Depends."

"Upon what?"

"Whether you're talking about driving or—" he sent her a soft smile "—something else."

"I was talking about driving."

"Are you sure?" His tone was lazy and confident as his arm tightened suggestively around her shoulders.

She should have bristled and let him know she was impervious to such flirtatious innuendos. Instead, she felt a quiver of excitement—and a warning.

When they reached the boardinghouse, Daylan parked the car as close to the front door as the small clearing in front would allow. All the windows of the house were dark except for the one in the small entrance hall. The rain was still coming down like an open faucet.

"Well, what do you think?" he said, turning toward her. "Shall we wait for it to stop?"

"And when do you think that might be?"

"Sometime after midnight, I'd wager. Would you care to make a bet?"

"No, thank you, cheater."

"What?" He gave her a look of mock indignation.

"You knew very well that Mrs. Duffy was cooking lamb stew for dinner before you bet me."

He laughed softly as he fingered a moist strand of hair drifting forward on her cheek. "Surely you don't think I have any inside track on the weather?" His face was dangerously close to hers.

She put a hand on his chest and lightly pushed him back. "I heard the same weather report you did— clearing by morning." His warm breath touched her face and she found it difficult to keep her voice light and airy. Her heart was suddenly doing weird things.

She felt vulnerable and a little frightened, as if her feelings were threatening to break free from the leash of her control.

She turned away, opened the door on her side and called over her shoulder as she bounded out, "Beat you to the house."

She was racing up the weathered steps of the house before he could maneuver his long legs out the driver's door and come around the car. Rainwater dripped off both of them, splashing on Mrs. Duffy's braided rug as they stood together in the small entrance hall.

"You could have waited for me to open an umbrella," he chided. He shed his rain slicker and slipped her raincoat from her shoulders. A line of pegs on the wall held similar garments, and several pairs of galoshes stood on the floor.

His hair was flattened like an ebony cap over his ears. Water ran down his cheek and nose, and droplets had collected on his thick eyebrows. He looked like a little boy who had stuck his head in a rain barrel.

"Are you laughing at me?" he demanded.

"Yes," she admitted with a broad grin, backing up as he playfully made a move toward her.

"For shame," he chided as he put two hands on the wall, one on each side of her. His eyes boldly traveled over her wet face and the damp sweater that clung to her breasts. She felt heat sweeping up into her glistening cheeks.

"It's yourself who must appease the jealous rain nymphs," he said, bending his face closer to hers. "Your beauty demands an offering," he whispered solemnly.

"Offering?" She tried for a teasing tone, but her voice was suddenly husky.

He smiled. "Yes."

"And if I ... don't want to make one?"

His fingertips slipped down her arms and drew her ever so slightly toward him. "But you do, don't you?" He parted his lips in a tantalizing way as his arms encircled her body.

She leaned into him. "Yes."

He lowered his mouth to hers and brushed her moist lips gently at first, then deepened the contact. Slowly the kiss built until it stirred a latent fire that pressed their bodies together in a flare of explosive desire. He worked the soft flesh of her lips, nibbling gently with his teeth and caressing her with his flickering tongue. Heat radiated through her body, and the water that trickled down her face from her drenched hair went unnoticed. She shivered, but not from cold.

Slowly he raised his mouth from hers and murmured in a thickened voice, "'Tis a rare colleen ye are, Maureen O'Mallory." He held her chin gently in his hand as he looked upon her face. "Sure and the velvet blue in yer eyes is like moonlight shining on the lapping waters of Lough Corrif. And the softest rosebud in Kilcarney wilts beside your lovely lips."

The poetic phrases were in harmony with his lilting brogue, and she was lost in a labyrinth of his touch and words. He captured her mouth in another long kiss.

When he drew away, she clung to him weakly, breathless and unsteady. He put his arm around her waist, and they walked up the narrow stairs together. She floated along beside him, wondering at the incredible delight her body experienced in his embrace.

Outside her door, he released his hold. She looked up at him. She knew her lips were warm and bruised and invited another kiss, but he stepped back and said rather formally without a trace of brogue, "Good night. See you in the morning, Maurie."

How could he do it? Shift back into the casual repartee they'd had before he shattered her emotions with his kisses and poetic murmurings? She felt a rejection that left her bewildered and a little frightened. Tears suddenly threatened to well up in her eyes.

"Good night," she managed in an uncertain tone. She turned away quickly, went into her room and closed the door. She stood there in the dark, biting her lip, until she heard his footsteps go on down the hall to his room. No man had ever devastated her with kisses the way he had. Her feelings had never skyrocketed with such burning desire as when she felt the firm length of his body pressed against hers. She'd always been in control of her emotions—until now.

Since coming to Ireland, she wasn't certain of anything.

Giving herself a mental shake, she straightened and firmed her shoulders. All right, so she was physically attracted to Daylan O'Shane. That didn't mean she couldn't keep a sensible rein on any romantic leanings in his direction. She'd seen the way he had flirted with the pretty cigarette girl. The quiver of jealousy she'd felt should have warned her even then that she was vulnerable to his easy charm.

Quickly she exchanged her damp clothes for a warm brushed-wool, floor-length nightgown. All the time she was preparing for bed, one of the Irish love songs Daylan had played in the car echoed in her head. She told herself she was much too sophisticated to fall for a smooth-talking Irishman whose behavior was as changeable as quicksilver.

As she pulled back the bedspread, a cold draft hit her back. Her head reeled and her chest was suddenly tight. Wind and rain battered the windowpane with the howl of a demented creature clawing to get in. Shadows moved out of the corners of the room. An uncontrollable shiver went through her as she stared at the bed.

A dead spray of tansy flowers lay in the middle of her pillow.

CHAPTER FOUR

The pungent odor of the withered flowers sent Maurie's head reeling. *Have a bit of tansy... for your bad dreams and all.* Maurie grabbed the yellow flowers and threw them into a wicker wastebasket. She frantically covered them up with trash but the pungent smell continued to invade the room.

Her breathing was shallow, her pulse thumped in her temples, and it was several moments before common sense came to her rescue and she was able to ridicule her emotional reaction. *What on earth is the matter with me?* She sat on the bed and brushed away the cold beads of perspiration on her forehead. Why did she feel helpless against some undefined power represented by an offensive little twig of tansy? A healthy, well-adjusted person would not react with such raw fear to a weird offering left on her pillow, she lectured herself. She'd never been susceptible to wild imaginings before. Why couldn't she keep her emotions under control now?

The strange little woman must have sneaked up to her room and left the sprig for her. It was as simple as that. Just the quirky action of someone who wasn't quite all there. All Maurie had to do was make certain that in the future her door was locked. That would stop any more peculiar offerings, she assured herself, even as some mocking inner voice questioned whether such a precaution would be effective.

Ireland seemed to be filled with eerie forces and bone-chilling superstitions. She remembered the scary story Daylan had told at dinner about trying to out-run the Women of Moher as they searched for the dead in a storm's thunder and lightning. The tale of his flight from the clutching furies had been a strange mixture of entertainment and confession. How much of it was true? She shivered now, just thinking about it.

The sound of the night wind filled the room with whispers. As rain ran in gray shadows down the pane, faces seemed to form and re-form against the glass. With a hasty jerk, she closed the homemade curtains. Her heartbeat sounded loudly in her ears for several minutes before she began to relax in the warm bed.

She picked up a textbook on American judges that she had promised herself to read during her leave of absence. Such a tedious subject would surely drive all fanciful thoughts from her mind, she told herself. But she gave up and turned out the light after she'd read the first page three times. Despite her valiant efforts, the events of the evening kept intruding.

She blushed to think of the way she had behaved on a first date. Daylan's poetic endearments sent her emotions reeling, and he'd fired every sense when he touched her. In a way, reality became strangely blurred when she was in his company. The resemblance between him and the horrid Oliver in her dream still lingered, even though she knew it was foolishness. The people in her nightmare were created by a strange quirking of her subconscious and nothing more. Undoubtedly Daylan was right. Though she couldn't remember it, she had seen the blond woman somewhere since her arrival in Ireland. And for some reason, she had fashioned the cruel Oliver with the same raven hair and brown-black eyes as Daylan.

What if I have the dream again tonight? Her body suddenly went rigid. She pulled the covers up around her neck as she lay wide-eyed in the narrow bed. The rain showed no sign of letting up as it peppered the slate roof and coated the windowpane. Gurgling water off the roof brought back the memory of the gargoyle with rainwater spilling out of its mouth. She recalled the scene from the high window, the expanse of green sloping ground and white-crested waves beating against a rocky shoreline. Her mouth went suddenly dry. Wasn't the nightmare ever going to fade? What if the dream came back the minute she fell asleep? What if she was drawn back into the horrible feeling of not being able to wake up?

She turned on the light again. If she'd been in her own apartment, she would have fixed a cup of cocoa and watched a late show until she became relaxed and drowsy. Sometimes, after a hard day of lectures, she was too keyed up to go right to sleep. But that was different. Never in her life had she been *afraid* to go to sleep.

Afraid? What nonsense! She scoffed at the idea. She wasn't lying wide-awake because she feared she would experience the same dream. And yet she waited, her body rigid against being unwittingly drawn into slumber. The rhythmic ticking of her travel clock mocked the slow passage of time.

The sound of the rain softened to a murmur and then faded into a hushed stillness. The storm was over. Daylan had been right. *Daylan. Daylan.* She spoke his name like an incantation until she unwittingly fell asleep.

Her hands nervously fingered the woolen coverlet when she awoke the next morning. She quickly looked around the room for reassurance that she was still in the boardinghouse bedroom. The night had passed without any disturbing dreams, and she laughed weakly with relief as she hopped out of bed and drew back the draperies.

A watery sunlight shone through a gauze of gray clouds, and rock fences and rolling hills were washed with a misty blue that could have come from a painter's wet brush. The air was soft and luminous, and Maurie's spirits rose as her gaze traveled over glistening hedges of yew and drooping wet willow branches.

She was in Ireland. Her pilgrimage to find her roots was about to begin.

She put on jeans and a loose-fitting pullover decorated with pale blue appliqué flowers. She combed one side of her hair behind her ear and fastened it with a clip, letting the other side fall softly free along her cheek. The style gave her face a jaunty carefree look and accented the alert lift of her eyebrows. She felt deliciously liberated from the staid life of a college professor.

When she entered the dining room, she was surprised to find she was the last of the boarders for breakfast. Mrs. Duffy was sitting at her end of the table, enjoying a second mug of coffee and reading a local newspaper.

Maurie apologized for being late.

The landlady brushed her apology aside. "Don't be giving it a thought. The Moreheads are off this morning on another sight-seeing trip. And Mr. O'Shane left early, too."

Maurie tried to deny that she felt disappointed at missing him, but her high spirits wavered a little as she sat down to eat across the table from his empty chair. She was curious as to whether he would have greeted her with a soft smile that hinted at the intimate scene in the hallway. Most likely he would have said good-morning with the same withdrawn manner as he had bade her good-night.

"I imagine you'll be wanting to take advantage of the bit of sunshine yerself," the landlady said as she served Maurie a bowl of mush floating in cream, followed by homemade sausage and light corn muffins.

"Yes, I'm glad the rain is over."

"For the moment," Mrs. Duffy said pessimistically. "Have some butter and honey with your muffins."

"I really shouldn't, but thanks." Every bite that Maurie took defeated her intention not to eat everything. "Delicious," she murmured, finally pushing back an empty plate. "I definitely need some exercise to work off food like this."

Mrs. Duffy nodded. "You've been cooped up for a couple of days. Do you good to get some fresh air."

"I think I'll walk into town. Where is the Catholic church located?"

Mrs. Duffy looked surprised. "You're a little late for early-morning mass."

"Oh, I'm not Catholic. I just want to talk to the priest—for my research." Maurie wasn't ready to provide the gossipy woman with details of her adoption by an American couple. No doubt the word would get out once she started making inquiries, but for the moment, she guarded her privacy.

"'Tis a nice little bicycle ride from here to the church. Yer welcome to use my wheels," Mrs. Duffy offered. "And I'll even send along a sandwich or two. Sure and the church is built in a nice little meadow, with a stream running through. 'Tis a nice day ye'll have for yerself."

"Thank you. I'll take you up on your offer of a bike. It'll be fun to see something of the country-side," Maurie said, eager to be out in the sun. She'd never realized how the lack of sunshine affected her moods.

She tied a sweater around her shoulders and set out on an old but serviceable bicycle with the sack containing her lunch resting in a wire basket. A bright sun beamed down from a clearing sky, drying up puddles in the country road and evaporating a lingering haze lying close to the ground. The smell of dank earth mingled with odors of wet wood, green moss and ferns.

Mrs. Duffy had suggested Maurie take the first lane that veered off to the left. "Ye'll bypass the town and save pedaling through the crowded streets along the quay."

Several times, Maurie wondered if she had taken the wrong path. The lane had been scarcely more than a gap in a waist-high hedgerow. She was cursing herself for not staying on the main road when she pedaled over a rise and saw a wide expanse of rolling ground crisscrossed by rock fences. Sheep were grazing on a nearby hill, and beyond them, on the horizon, the steeple of a church and the rooftops of the town rose against the sky.

The church was farther away than it looked, and Maurie was puffing by the time she reached the small structure made of gray stones, fashioned with a belfry and a white cross pointing the way to heaven. Parking her bicycle near a rusted gate, she paused and looked around. She was perspiring slightly so she took the sweater off her shoulders and left it in the narrow basket. Should she enter the church or try the rectory that stood a short distance behind the church? Since she saw no indication that services were being conducted, she walked down a narrow path to the rectory, climbed three weathered steps and knocked on the door.

A middle-aged woman with a mop in her hands answered the door. She wore a black dress covered by a white bib apron. Her bold black eyes took in Maurie's designer jeans and fashionable pullover, and the lines around her mouth tightened. She gave Maurie a short bob of her gray-black head. "What are ye wanting, miss?"

"I'm sorry to bother you," Maurie began apologetically, "but it's important that I speak with Father Flynn. Is he here?"

The woman's eyes widened. Then she gave a snort that might have been amusement or disgust. "Ye'll find him over yonder." She shifted the mop to her other gnarled hand and pointed.

Maurie turned her head. The woman was pointing at the graveyard. Nothing but gray tombstones marked the flat ground that stretched between the church and the rectory.

"He's . . . ?"

"Gone these eleven years, God rest his soul."

Maurie knew she shouldn't have been surprised, but disappointment was evident in her face as she turned back to the housekeeper. "I'm sorry. I didn't know."

"American, ain't ye?" Her tone indicated she had little use for tourists wandering about asking questions.

Maurie nodded. "Yes, I arrived a couple of days ago. I'm staying with Mrs. Duffy." She watched the woman's face to see if the landlady's name might lend a touch of respectability to her presence at the church.

The woman's expression never wavered. "Why are ye asking after Father Flynn?" she demanded.

Maurie wasn't about to tell the housekeeper her business. She didn't like her hostile attitude, and her sharp eyes held no sincere interest in being helpful. "Perhaps I could speak with someone else?"

"Ain't nobody here but me and Father Sashoney."

Maurie returned the woman's belligerent stare. "Then I would like to speak with Father Sashoney."

The housekeeper's eye fell to Maurie's muddy ankle-high boots. "I don't take to people messing up my floor just when I finished mopping. Wait in front of the church. Maybe he'll come and speak to you there." Her tone implied that maybe he wouldn't.

She shut the door and Maurie was left staring at the weathered boards wondering if she should knock again. The woman hadn't even taken her name, not that it would mean anything to the priest. Maybe she would have to write a letter to Father Sashoney and ask for an appointment.

Maurie turned away reluctantly and had almost reached the front of the church when she heard a door open and close at the rectory. She turned around. A young priest came down the front steps, a black tunic whipping around his long legs. He was frowning as he strode quickly down the path toward her.

Maurie waited, feeling a sense of relief. She was going to get to talk with someone, after all.

The white clerical collar around the young priest's neck hung rather loosely under a protruding Adam's apple, and his clerical garb showed signs of a poor alteration. His face was too lean and his features too irregular to be attractive. "Homely" was the word that came to Maurie's mind as she looked at him. She was surprised to find his voice brisk and rather pompous for one so young.

"I'm Father Sashoney," he told her, and without waiting for her to return the introduction, he said, "My housekeeper told me you were asking for Father Flynn. I gather she told you he is deceased?"

"Yes. Thank you for taking the time to speak with me. I'm Maureen Miller, from the United States." She stuck out her hand for a shake.

His hand was uncertain in hers and accompanied by another frown. "Yes?"

"I'm seeking information, which you may be able to give me." She used a professional tone that matched his.

"What kind of information?"

"Is there someplace where we may talk?"

He nodded toward an iron bench near one of the rock walls that edged the graveyard. When they were seated she explained that she was seeking information about her parentage. "I was adopted as an infant by an American couple. I know that my mother's name was Maelene O'Mallory. I also know from a letter written by Father Flynn to my adoptive father that the priest was in touch with my mother at the time of the adoption. I've come to Ireland to find out as much as I can about the circumstances of my birth."

"In most cases it can do no harm, but in others..." His homely face became solemn.

Maurie ignored the warning in his voice. "The truth is always better than living with a lot of unanswered questions," she argued. "Since I can't obtain any information from Father Flynn, perhaps there are records?"

"The home and small orphanage run by our Catholic sisters closed down nearly a dozen years ago." A shadow crossed the young priest's eyes as he studied her. "Perhaps it is better not to stir the ashes of the past."

The skin on her neck began to prickle. "What do you mean?"

He quoted sonorously, "'Our birth is nothing but our death begun. As tapers waste the moment they take fire.'" She was certain he used the same voice when offering a requiem.

"Do you know something about my background—something you think I shouldn't know?"

He fingered the cross hanging on his chest. "The sisters took in only the most unfortunate of cases. I warn you that stories about the abandoned young women who sought sanctuary with them are not pleasant."

Maurie moistened her dry lips. "I am prepared to face the truth."

"Take my advice. Go home. I warn you that your life will not be enriched by this quest of yours. You should content yourself with the blessings that God has given you—and be grateful for them."

His patronizing tone sparked her temper. "The Lord has also given me the courage to know the truth," she countered, determined not to be put off by his sanctimonious manner. "I understand the church has always taken care to record marriages, births and deaths. Surely there are records of adoptions, as well."

"All the records were taken away, and I'm not sure if they are still in existence. Or where they might be stored."

"Isn't there someone who would know?"

"I can make some inquiries, but that will take time. The priest who took over from Father Flynn passed away a year ago and I'm quite new to the parish."

"I would appreciate any inquiries you might make." She stood up and thanked the young priest for his time. "I'll be anxious to hear from you." She told him where she was staying.

He nodded. "Mrs. Duffy is one of our faithful parishioners." For some reason that seemed to put a plus in her column, thought Maurie.

"Where was the home and orphanage located?" she asked.

For a moment she thought he was going to refuse to answer. Then he pointed. "Just over that next rise. Not much left to mark the spot. Everything has fallen into ruin. The buildings are just piles of rock. A small overgrown cemetery is the only thing that remains. You'll not find any peace of mind there," he said flatly.

She thanked him again, retrieved the bike and pushed off in the direction he'd indicated. She felt his solemn eyes biting into her back as the warning edge to his voice lingered in her ears. *You'll not find any peace of mind there.*

The road was nothing more than a rutted path, and the rocky hillside was steep. She stood up on the pedals as she made the laborious ascent. Rainwater had collected in puddles and she did her best to maneuver around them. Her back tire slipped dangerously, and several times she nearly sprawled sideways before she caught herself with one foot and righted the bike.

When she reached the top of the rise, she was breathing heavily. She stopped and brushed moist hair back from her eyes. The barren land rolled away, bleak and desolate. Piles of tumbled rocks marked the places where the buildings had stood, and half-buried markers of gray stones defined the boundaries of a small graveyard.

She began to tremble. The hauntingly empty scene stabbed her with rising emotion. As she stood there she could hear wails of babies carried on the wind. Moans of pain lingered in the eerie silence. She wanted to cry out to some unseen force sweeping over her. A sob rose in her throat. As if the piles of stones and the barren ground held the spirits of those who had spilled their lifeblood in this haunted place, she felt them reaching out to her.

Abandoning the bike, she walked slowly across the harsh, thistle-covered ground toward the first row of gray tombstones. The earth and sky met in a swirl of light before her eyes. Dry bracken crackled under her feet. When she reached the first sunken tombstone, she dropped to her knees, brushed aside wild growth in front of the simple stone and read the inscribed name and date: "BABY DONOVAN. Born and Died August 12, 1958."

A deep sadness flowed over her as she moved to the next grave, and the next. She pulled weeds and scraped dirt away from each small chiseled stone. All the names were those of young women or children.

Propelled by a mounting compulsion she couldn't control, she moved from one line of graves to the next. Her fingers were scratched and bleeding as she cleared each stone. Her back and arms ached. Tears blurred her vision. With only a half-dozen graves remaining, she found the tombstone she was looking for. Half-buried in a tangle of thistles, an inscribed stone bore the name MAELENE O'MALLORY.

A cry broke free from her throat as she knelt down beside the grave and fixed her eyes on the dates that showed that Maelene had been seventeen when she died—three days after Maurie's birth.

Tears spilled out of Maurie's eyes and down her dusty cheeks. She began to pull away the brambles and coarse grass with a fury that was a release for her emotions. When the mound was cleared and embedded dirt removed from the letters on the weathered stone, Maurie's brow was beaded with sweat and her hands were raw.

She bowed her head, closed her eyes and let the past seep into her mind. Her mother had come to the Catholic sisters because she was going to have a child. Father Flynn had not mentioned the natural father's name in his letter, so he either didn't know who fathered the child or had chosen not to reveal the name. The baby had been delivered and put up for adoption. And her mother had died. Only a few days after delivery.

Utter desolation overwhelmed Maurie. The wind quickened, rushing across the ground. Even in the bright sunlight, she was suddenly cold. Her energy was gone, and a bone-deep weariness overtook her. She buried her face in her hands and wept for the mother she had never known. Her weeping brought release, and after a few moments, she felt calm.

She brushed away her tears, lowered her hands from her face. A shadowy green light fell around her as a canopy of trees overhead shielded her from the sun. The barren graveyard had disappeared. She was no longer beside her mother's grave but sitting on a wrought-iron bench in the shade of a beech tree.

The little girl, Hollie, was playing at her feet with toys scattered on the lush green grass around her.

CHAPTER FIVE

A sickening shiver crept down her spine. The nightmare! She was dreaming again. The terror she had felt before rushed over her. *Wake up. Wake up!* She fought against being drawn into an existence that wasn't her own. It was horrible to be trapped, knowing she was dreaming and not being able to stop it. The sound of crashing waves vibrated in her ears and the smell of the ocean filled her nostrils. Why was everything so real?

Shadows absorbed slivers of sunlight piercing the thick grid of tree branches overhead. No warmth from the sun reached Maurie as she sat in the shade of the huge tree. On every side heavy growth blotted out the view except for the one directly in front of her. Sheer cliffs dropped away to jagged rocks below, and white ocean spumes pounded and sucked like greedy tongues upon the jagged coastline. The earth appeared to crumple away with each relentless assault and the ground under her feet vibrated with the danger.

Why was she trapped in this place? A strangled scream rose in her throat. *It couldn't be happening. Not again.*

"Mama . . . Mama." Little fingers pulled at her floral skirt.

Maurie looked down into the child's face. The little girl's round azure eyes and rich brown hair matched her own. Ice froze in Maurie's veins. Her mouth went dry. *She looks like me.*

For a long moment, the little girl stared back at Maurie. Then her face puckered and she gave a shrill wail. On wobbly legs, she fled across the lawn, crying and reaching out for her nanny, who was standing a short distance away.

"What is it, Hollie, dear?"

The child screamed, pointed back at Maurie and then hugged the nanny's legs.

"Hush, hush," the motherly woman soothed as she lifted the child up into her arms. She spoke to a gray-haired man who was standing beside her.

He was lean, round shouldered, and wearing over-size glasses on his aquiline nose. They both turned and looked across the lawn at Maurie, and as the man fixed unblinking eyes upon her, she felt a wave of animosity rolling toward her. She saw with a start that he carried a doctor's bag.

Like the roar of thunder and the flash of lightning, an explosion of raw fear burst into Maurie's head. She had to get away! She pushed against the bench with her hands, trying to get up, but her leg muscles refused to stiffen enough to raise her to her feet. Her limbs and feet were cold despite the warmth of a knitted afghan lying across her lap. The palms of her hands were moist with hot sweat.

Can you die in a dream? Sobs rose in her throat. She felt ill. Why couldn't she wake up? A fiercely beating heart pounded in her ears. Why was she trapped in this horrible nightmare? Danger swirled around her like a devil's wind.

The frowning nanny sent Maurie a disparaging look and then disappeared with the child down a stone walk that wound through a thick stand of poplar and beech. The doctor walked over to Maurie.

"Good morning, Dawna. How are we feeling today?" he asked in a crisp professional tone.

I'm not Dawna. Maurie closed her eyes. This isn't happening. I won't be a part of this horrible nightmare another minute. "I am Maurie Miller. Maurie Miller."

She must have spoken aloud for he ordered sharply, "Stop it, Dawna. Stop that nonsense this minute." His expression was totally without warmth, without understanding. Gray eyes looking at her through dark-rimmed glasses were like iced pewter. He set down his bag. Gold letters were imprinted on the leather. Thomas A. Ferges, M.D.

"These spells of yours seemed to be increasing."

Maurie jerked her hand away from the fingers he put on her wrist. She sent a silent, frantic plea to the man staring down at her with a dark, closed face. *Please . . . please. Let me go.*

He grabbed her hand again, more forcefully this time. "Behave yourself, Dawna."

She bit her lip as he held her wrist and fixed his gaze on his watch. Then he shook his head. "Rapid, much too rapid. Not good at all. Now what's the matter? Why won't you cooperate? All of this stress is unnecessary. What is going on in that odd mind of yours?"

"I don't know." Her voice trembled. "I want to wake up and I can't."

"I have to warn you that your husband is concerned about your behavior. Even your own child is afraid of you."

She's not my child. The protest was a silent scream in her throat. What if she told him the truth? *She's afraid of me because I'm not her mother.* Maurie searched the doctor's face. His expression was closed, unreadable.

"I've had a talk with your husband, Dawna. We both agree that unless there is some improvement in your behavior, we will place you in less comfortable surroundings." His eyes remained distant as he made the veiled threat.

"What do you mean?"

"There are people who know how to handle irrational behavior like yours. Maybe you've been pampered too much, Dawna. Time for you to face up to reality."

Maurie closed her eyes. *I don't know what's happening. Why I'm dreaming all this.*

He gave a dismissing wave of his hand. "Why won't you make it easy on yourself, Dawna, and adhere to Oliver's wishes? He's your husband and he's been more than patient. But this stubbornness of yours has pushed him to the limit of his endurance. I warn you, you must give in to Oliver or suffer the consequences."

Oliver. She remembered clearly the cold arrogant Oliver Fitzgerald. Even a weird nightmare could not suppress the anger that suddenly flared. She didn't know why Dawna was being manipulated or threatened by her husband and this frigid doctor, but she cried furiously, "If you're Dawna's doctor, why aren't you looking out for her welfare? You should be protecting her. She's your patient. You're treating her like the enemy."

Too late she realized she'd made a terrible mistake. Her anger and open resistance had only heightened the doctor's malevolent expression.

"Don't you understand?" she said in a conciliatory tone. "I'm not Dawna! Oliver isn't my husband. And Hollie is the only one who recognizes the truth."

"And what is the truth?" he asked as softly as the flick of a rapier.

Her voice trembled. "I'm caught in the web of a horrible dream and I can't wake up."

He just looked at her for a long moment and then he opened his black bag. With an unhurried movement he filled a syringe.

"No," she said, cowering.

"Nurse," he called.

The blond Miss Doughty appeared quickly, as if she'd been waiting nearby. Her appearance was the same as before—white uniform and pink sweater, blond hair pulled back at the nape of her neck. She held Maurie's arm firmly as the doctor injected the needle.

"That will settle her down," he said, closing his bag. "If these tantrums continue, we'll make arrangements to have her moved." He pursed his narrow lips. "Something more has to be done to gain her cooperation."

"Come on, Dawna," the nurse said. "Time to go back to bed."

Maurie heard the doctor say something, but the words came to her from a distance. Already her head was beginning to feel light. She was aware of the nurse's and doctor's hands under her armpits as they lifted her up.

She cried out. Frantically her hands reached out, clutching at anything for support. With a burst of light, the dizziness faded as quickly as it had come. Her eyes flew open. Full sunlight hit her face as she lay forward across her mother's grave. One cheek was pressed against the ground and her fingers had dug into the dirt. She lay there without moving. Shaken. Her heart thumping loudly in her ears. Terror lay on her moist skin.

I must have fallen asleep. Tired from the strenuous bicycle ride and the emotional strain of finding her mother's grave, she had been lulled into taking a nap—and the horrible nightmare had come back.

Slowly she raised her head and looked around. The deserted scene was the same, the ground covered with bracken and brittle weeds, mounds of gray stones lying where they had fallen. Anything worth carrying off had disappeared long ago. Nothing of the living remained. Only the dead still claimed possession of the desolate knoll. For a moment, terror was there again. She couldn't shake off the trapped feeling of the dream.

She rose to her feet and started walking back toward the place where she had left the bike. As she passed a tumbled heap of stones that might have been the front wall of the home, the wind lifted dirt from the dusty ground. At the same moment, the pungent smell of tansy assaulted her nostrils. She froze. Spun around.

The wizened little woman who called herself Tansie stood in the shambles of the fallen walls. Her gray corkscrew curls sprang wildly away from the scarf she had tied around her head, and she wore the same shapeless sweater, dark pants and black scuffed boots. She clutched a straggly bouquet of yellow button flowers, and as she walked toward Maurie, she said, "A bit of tansy for your dreams. To help you find your way, Maurie."

"Stay away from me!" Maurie backed up. Had the woman put a spell on her? She brushed a hand across her eyes. *Am I awake . . . or dreaming?*

She desperately drew on the reality her senses provided. The barren knoll with its tumbled stones was real. The taste of dust was on her lips and the feel of wind was on her cheeks. The woman had called her Maurie, so she must be herself. Maurie's bewilderment was suddenly laced with anger. She clenched her fists. "Quit harassing me. Quit following me. And stay out of my room!"

She turned and stumbled back to her bicycle. She pedaled at a dangerous speed down the hill, past the church and along the narrow lane that led back the way she'd come. When the boardinghouse came into view, she slowed her flight.

Impulsively she turned into a footpath at the edge of the property and rode down a gentle slope to a wooded area only a short distance from the house. She let the bike drop and she lowered herself to the ground, leaning back against a twisted tree trunk. She didn't dare return to the house with Mrs. Duffy's lunch uneaten.

For a long time, she just sat there, getting her breath and letting the events of the morning wash over her. In the cemetery she'd been drawn back into the horrible nightmare. The same people had been in the dream— the nanny, the little girl and the nurse. And the doctor . . . what was his name? She tried to remember, but the gold-lettered words she'd seen on his bag wouldn't form in her memory. She shook herself. *Stop it! Let the dream die in the subconscious.*

She opened the lunch sack and gave her attention to a generous mustard mutton sandwich, a hard-boiled egg and a thermos of cold milk. Eating slowly, she let her gaze wander over a nearby field where a dozen cows grazed lazily. A dog barked somewhere in the distance. The boardinghouse and green barn were a part of the tranquil scene. At the bottom of a gentle slope was a thick stand of beech, willow and poplar fed by a small stream. An insidious fear that she might fall asleep again kept her body rigid. Even a short nap might draw her back into the nightmare where she was no longer Maureen Miller but someone called Dawna. The second dream had been as disturbing as the first one—and just as real.

She had just finished her lunch when she saw someone come out the back door of the house and cross the field that lay between her and the house. At first she wasn't certain who it was and then her heart quickened. Daylan. She was about to get up and wave to him when he veered sharply to the left and disappeared into the stand of trees.

He must be going for a walk. Eager to join him, she headed after him. In a minute she was in a tunnel of trees that hugged the wandering stream. She followed the water a short distance and then stopped. No sign of Daylan. She was afraid she'd only lose her way if she went any deeper into the woods.

Hot and thirsty, she knelt down beside the stream and splashed her face, delighting in the shocking chill that prickled her skin. She washed the dried blood from her scratched hands. She was still on her knees when she heard footsteps somewhere behind her. She swung her head around, searching the dark green shadows. A second later, a quiver of movement was followed by the crunch of deadfall. Two men came into view, pushing aside some lower branches as they moved forward.

A surprised gasp caught soundless in her throat. One of them was Daylan O'Shane. His visage was darkly solemn, and something furtive and threatening in his manner kept her silent. With the instinct of a frightened doe, she froze, still kneeling beside the stream. She waited. A nearby fallen log crusted with moss gave her some concealment.

The two men passed by without seeing her and stopped a short distance downstream as if waiting. A moment later she saw another man coming from the other direction. As the three men stood and talked, Maurie could hear the hushed murmur of their voices but couldn't understand what they were saying. The two men wore dark caps set forward on their heads so that the brims shaded their eyes. Both were large and burly and dressed in coarse worn clothes. One had a full black beard. Whatever Daylan was telling them only increased the ugly scowls on their faces. The bearded one made an angry slicing motion with his hand.

Maurie's mouth went dry. If Daylan and the other men retraced their steps, she might not be as lucky as she was the first time they had passed her. The intensity of their rendezvous warned her she could be in danger if they found her cowering a few feet away.

Remaining in a hunched position, she quietly moved away from the stream, intent on going back the way she had come as quickly as possible. She breathed a sigh of relief when she made it out of the trees and fled up the grassy knoll to where she had eaten lunch.

Grabbing the thermos, she threw it into the bicycle's wire basket and was about to take off when a movement from behind stopped her.

Daylan lurched around in front of the bike and put his hand firmly on the handlebars. He planted his feet to keep her from moving. His dark eyes held chips of red fire. A growl came deep from within his chest. "What in the hell do you think you're doing spying on me!"

CHAPTER SIX

Angry shadows darkened his eyes, and his voice was hard as flint. "What are you doing spying on me?" he repeated.

His accusing tone brought Maurie's chin up in a defiant lift. She wasn't going to be badgered by him or anyone else. His manner sparked her anger. She wasn't the one who should be offering explanations.

"Let go of my bike."

He glared at her for a moment, then removed his hands from the handlebars. "We have to talk. Why were you eavesdropping?"

"I wasn't," she said in a reasonable tone, hoping the nervous trembling in her stomach didn't show. She'd been battered on too many levels that morning. The cemetery...the nightmare...Tansie. And now this confrontation. She felt betrayed by Daylan's behavior and anger. Absurd as it was, he had represented some kind of anchor in the turmoil that had engulfed her since her arrival in Ireland.

She let the bike drop and walked over to the place where she had eaten her lunch. A couple of pretty skylarks were pecking enthusiastically at scraps of bread she'd tossed away from her lunch. The cows were still lowing in the field and the unseen dog kept up its barking. Everything was the same—and yet terribly different. With a further spark of defiance, she turned to him. "I think you owe me an explanation."

For a moment he just looked at her, a tightening quirking at the corner of his mouth. Then his mouth softened. "I was about to say the same thing."

"You first. What were you doing with those...those raunchy-looking men."

"Having a meeting," he answered readily. His eyes narrowed. "Of course, you know that from your spying."

"I couldn't hear what was being said, but it looked...nefarious."

His mouth eased into a mocking smile, but his eyes remained guarded and shadowed. "Nefarious? Now that's an interesting word."

"I assume you know what it means?" she answered tartly in her professor's tone.

He laughed then, eased himself to the ground and pulled her down beside him. "Well, I guess I'll have to confess. I'm trying to pull off a lucrative business deal."

"Business? With those men? What kind?"

"Among other things, I'm a textile broker," he said smoothly. "I buy lace made by women in their cottages and sell it to large industries who market them worldwide."

"But why all the secrecy?"

"I was contacted by some unscrupulous men who control the female workers in this area, and I agreed to meet with them. I didn't want anyone to see me in their company. I'm sorry I let my temper get away from me. When I saw you slinking away from your hiding place, I overreacted. I apologize. Now it's your turn. What were you doing hiding behind that log?"

"I wasn't hiding exactly. I mean, I saw you when you left the house. I thought you were taking a walk and I wanted to join you. When I saw you with those men . . ." Her voice trailed off.

"Yes? And what are you accusing me of?"

In retrospect her reaction had been melodramatic to say the least. How could she explain the sense of danger that had come over her? Even at a distance she had felt the intensity of emotion in the exchange between the three men. Was it her imagination? She wanted to believe him. After all, what did she know about the undercurrents of doing business in this strange land?

"I'm sorry. I guess I overreacted, too." She took a deep breath as her gaze traveled over the quiet pastoral scene. All apprehension dissipated, and as she sat beside him, she was filled with contentment.

He gently turned her chin in his direction, bringing his lips tantalizingly close to hers. "I said I was sorry. Can't we kiss and make up?"

Without waiting for consent, his mouth captured hers tenderly yet possessively, teasing her lips into soft surrender. She was breathless when he drew back, his eyes soft and caressing.

She wanted to laugh for no sensible reason. He took her hand and frowned when he saw the scratches. "What have you been doing to your hands?"

His concern radiated companionship, sharing and understanding. With relief, she told him about her visit to the church.

"Father Flynn is no longer alive, and frankly, I didn't care for the dour young priest in charge. He offered me very little information, and I had the feeling he thought my inquiries to be inappropriate."

"Maybe he just doesn't like Americans," offered Daylan. "Or maybe he has too many other things on his mind."

"He said he'd inquire about the records from the sisters' home and orphanage."

"Well, then, why the bereft look in those lovely blue eyes?"

Her lower lip trembled. "I went to the place where the home and orphanage had been. Nothing's left but rubble and the cemetery. That's where I got the scratches. I had to clear weeds from most of the gravestones before I found my mother's." Her eyes welled with tears. "She died three days after my birth."

Daylan drew Maurie close, reached in his pocket and gave her a generous blue handkerchief. She blew her nose and wiped her eyes. When she had regained her composure, she apologized. "I'm sorry. I didn't mean to give in like that."

He gently brushed back the hair from her moist cheeks. Holding her against his chest, his lips touched her forehead with a tender kiss. "You're sure you found the right grave? I mean, it might be a different O'Mallory."

"No, it's the only Maelene buried there. And the dates match. Besides, I know I was adopted from that orphanage because of Father Flynn's letter to my adoptive parents. There's no mistake."

She was about to tell Daylan about the recurring nightmare and Tansie's unexpected appearance when he pulled away from her. "Now you've found out what you wanted to know, I think you should leave Ireland. There is nothing but pain for you here."

She stiffened, startled by his directness. She felt an invisible barrier suddenly mounted between them. His manner was crisp and blunt. One minute he caressed her with all the tenderness of a lover and the next advised her to go away. Was he warning her? Did he think she would mistake a casual flirtation for a serious commitment? Her pride smarted. "I'll leave when I'm ready."

She jerked to her feet, confused and hurt. Hot indignation sparked her eyes as she stood up and glared down at him. He just sat there, staring pensively into the distance as she picked up the bike and rode off.

* * *

Daylan didn't show up at suppertime, and Maurie spent the evening listening to the Moreheads talk about their sight-seeing tour while Mrs. Duffy sat in her rocker, plying her tatting needle. Maurie stared into a brightly burning turf fire and searched her mind for some rationale that would make sense of the day's happenings.

She was certain now that Daylan hadn't told her the truth. How could she have accepted for one instant his story about the reason for meeting with those two disreputable-looking men? He had lied to her. Boldly. Without conscience. The more she thought about her gullibility, the more furious she was with herself for being taken in. From now on, she decided, she would be on guard. No telling what was going on with him. She'd been warned that Ireland was a country of conflict and smoldering hatred. Was Daylan a part of it? She shivered, remembering the cold hatred in his eyes when he'd spoken about the death of his sister.

"I believe I'll call it a day," she said, getting to her feet. "My eyes are getting a little heavy."

"No better exercise than riding a bike," Mrs. Duffy said with a nod. "You'll sleep like a baby tonight, I'll wager."

"I hope you're right," Maurie answered and then as a familiar panic jolted her she added, "But sometimes you can be too tired and sleep won't come."

"Mr. O'Shane kept you out pretty late last night," said Mrs. Morehead with a knowing smirk. "I heard you pass my door." She gave an amused chuckle. "He must be quite the ladies' man. He's out in the evening a lot."

"Yes, isn't he," Maurie said with a catch in her throat.

"Business, I think," offered Mrs. Duffy.

"What kind of business is he in?" Maurie asked as casually as she could. "He said he was a peddler, but what does he peddle?"

The landlady frowned. "Don't know exactly. Anyway, he told me he'd be gone in the evenings and might even be away a day or two from time to time. He paid me extra to hold his room for him."

Mrs. Morehead nodded. "I remember when Mr. Morehead was on the road." As she launched into a long recital of her husband's travels, Maurie slipped upstairs to her room.

She took her toiletries into the large, old-fashioned bathroom and ran a tub of wonderfully warm water. After soaking for a long spell, she reluctantly climbed out into the invigoratingly chilly room and dried off with a sweet-smelling towel. Back in her room, she dressed in a pair of velour pajamas, then brushed her hair until it snapped.

For one brief moment her stomach tightened as she turned down the covers on her bed. Then with a short laugh, she let out her breath. No tansy offerings like the night before.

Her uneasiness made her feel utterly foolish. How could she have let a bizarre little woman affect her so? Obviously the woman had some kind of a fixation on her. Following her around. Handing her a tansy bouquet. The unexpected way she had appeared at the cemetery had been most unnerving. Maurie was glad she had told her to quit bothering her. Her life was in enough of a tailspin.

One thing was clear—her feelings for Daylan O'Shane were far beyond the boundaries of common sense. When his mesmerizing dark eyes looked into hers, she was swamped with a desire that raced hotly into the deepest core of her being. No man had ever caused such a whirlwind of emotions. Even now, her whole body remembered the feel of him, the heat of his touch. The spicy smell of his skin remained with her, and the urgency of his mouth on hers brought a quivering tremble to her stomach. She tried to put him out of her thoughts, but there was no way to ignore her tangled emotions.

She lay in bed with her eyes wide open. Time ticked by slowly. All semblance of sleep evaded her. She turned restlessly in the bed.

Swearing, she turned on her light and tried to read. Even the latest *New York Times* bestseller failed to hold her attention, and she finally turned off her light again.

The luminous dial on her traveling clock showed midnight.

Then one o'clock. Two o'clock.

She told herself firmly that she wasn't waiting for Daylan's measured steps in the hall, nor was she afraid to go to sleep. Dreams, however real, were a flight of the imagination, a trick played by the subconscious, she reassured herself, and lots of people had recurring nightmares. She wished she had read more about dream interpretation. There must be some rational reason for why she was fantasizing about being someone called Dawna. And why the overriding sense of danger and menace in her dream? She'd always felt secure in her rather mundane life; there was no personal or professional crisis she couldn't handle. Her health was good, and her energy level had always been high. The kind of fear she experienced in her nightmare was as foreign to her as the helplessness that came to her as Dawna.

None of it made sense. An icy chill went through Maurie as she lay there, knowing that the nightmare was waiting to engulf her again. She turned over on her side, determined to keep her thoughts centered on pleasant things, such as her cat, Buzzie. A wash of homesickness overtook her. She missed the cat's soft fur and his comforting purring as he kneaded the bed covers and found a soft spot in the curve of her legs.

She had left the draperies open, and she watched tiny gray clouds like a school of baby whales float

across the moon. She thought she heard water running, and it reminded her of the small stream in the
wood where Daylan had met with the two men.

The memory returned clearly, the way he had stood
with his back to her, the dark cap of hair curling on his
neck. The faces of the two strangers were sharp in her
mind. The biggest one had a bulbous nose above a
thick black beard. The other man was shorter, thick
shouldered, and she could see his eyes clearly as he
held his cap in his hand.

"You bloody well better make sure!" Daylan said,
shaking a threatening finger at them.

"Ain't nothing going wrong," the bearded man
snapped.

"If there's any trouble, we know what to do." The
bull-like man made a slice across his neck.

"We'll be needing some money."

With a guttural oath, he went around the desk and
jerked open a drawer—Maurie's breath caught in her
throat. Desk. Furniture. Mullioned windows. She
wasn't watching the scene from behind a tree trunk
now. She was looking through a small crack in the
bathroom door that opened into Oliver Fitzgerald's
sitting room.

"You'll get the rest when the job's done." Oliver's
black mustache made a hard line above his mouth as
he handed them the money. "And you're fish bait if
there's a foul-up."

"Sure thing, Mr. Fitzgerald. And about your wife..." A sudden rush of air hit the back of Maurie's neck. Rough hands swung her around. She felt a blow on the side of her head. A dark fog rolled over her as she went down.

The silence was broken by a loud whimpering. She turned her head on the pillow, clutched the covers and fought the icy chill that had invaded her limbs. When she opened her eyes the luminous dial of her clock met her eyes. Three-fifteen.

With a sob she sat up in bed. The side of her head throbbed, and as she gingerly touched the spot she felt a bump rising above her right ear.

The old house creaked and she heard the plaintive cry of a night bird like the whimper of a child. The whimper came again and she realized that the sound was coming from her own throat.

She trembled and hugged herself fiercely as her mind and body threatened to shatter like porcelain dashed upon hard stone. The erratic fierce pounding of her heart sounded loudly in her ears. Was it Daylan or Oliver she had seen with the same two men? Was she awake now—or dreaming? She bit her lower lip hard, as if the pain was somehow reassuring. Oliver seemed more real to her now than Daylan. Pressing her fingertips against her temple, she sought to drive out the overlapping imprints on her mind.

Was this madness?

Were Daylan and Oliver the same man? Was she experiencing two sides of the same personality? Oliver—cold ... demanding ... threatening. And Daylan—hiding his cruel other self in overtures of passion and desire?

She clutched the covers high around her neck. Outside, the wind quickened with a mournful wail and the gray clouds thickened against the moon. As she lay there stiff with fear and dread, the faint scent of tansy touched her nostrils.

CHAPTER SEVEN

Morning finally came and a dull gray light invaded the room. A sleepless night had put violet shadows under Maurie's eyes, her head felt heavy and her eyes burned. She wondered if she were physically ill. *Or is the sickness just in my mind?*

Her every movement was leaden as she dressed and went through her morning ritual. She was downstairs before Mrs. Duffy had stoked the fire in the stove.

"Begorra, 'tis an early bird you are this mornin'," the landlady greeted Maurie. "And looking a wee bit peaked, I might say."

"I...I couldn't sleep."

"Is there something wrong with the bed?"

"Oh, no. The bed's fine."

"Are you warm enough? There's a chill in the house these April nights. I could bring in another comforter if you're sleeping cold."

Maurie shook her head, remembering the hot sweat that had coated her body last night. How could she explain to this practical, no-nonsense woman that she was afraid to go to sleep, afraid that she would lose herself in a nightmare that was as real as anything she had ever experienced? "Everything's fine," she lied, her mouth suddenly dry as the memory of the horrible nightmare came back.

Mrs. Duffy gave her an odd look, as if Maurie's expression had spoken louder then her words. She pursed her lips, opened her mouth and then closed it again. Shrugging, the older woman turned away and busied herself at the stove.

Maurie slumped down in a kitchen chair.

"A nice cup of coffee will set things right," Mrs. Duffy said briskly.

Maurie wanted to confide in her, but the words wouldn't come. The Irish landlady was too practical, too down to earth. How could she expect anyone to understand what was happening? *I'm having nightmares...where I become someone else. And I'm afraid. Something terrible is going to happen to that other me.*

No, she couldn't talk to Mrs. Duffy. And there was no one else. If she'd been at home, she would have sought out a friend of hers, an elderly gentleman in the psychology department. Professor Deburg would have offered a sensible perspective on the whole disturbing experience. But Professor Deburg was in the United States and she was on the other side of the Atlantic in Glenmara, Ireland.

The only person she'd met who might offer her some counseling was Father Sashoney. She hadn't been particularly taken with the young priest's personality, but at the moment, the father's charm was of little consequence. She just needed some knowledgeable person to tell her what she already knew—that the dream was only a dream. Sharing her anxiety with someone like a Catholic priest would surely put an end to the schizophrenic torture.

After breakfast, she borrowed Mrs. Duffy's bicycle and pedaled to the church. Clouds were gathering darkly on the horizon and the smell of rain was in the air. An urgency she couldn't quite define matched the ominous threat of the approaching storm. She pedaled down the narrow road and passed a few people carrying baskets and sacks as if heading for some kind of farmer's market. They stared at her as she went past, but none of them returned her hasty greeting. Once a woolly dog ran out and nipped at her feet until an old man called him back.

When she reached the church, she left the bike leaning against the same rock wall as before and walked down the stone path to the rectory. Since it was quite early, she was certain she'd find Father Sashoney at home. But she was wrong.

"He ain't here," said the same crusty housekeeper. She wore the same gray dress and big apron. This time she had a dish towel in her hand instead of a broom. "Was called out in the night, he was." She scowled at Maurie. "What do you want him for? He told you yesterday he didn't know nothing about that woman, Maelene O'Mallory."

The way she spat out the name startled Maurie. Her mouth went dry as she asked, "Do you know something about her?"

"Humph!" The woman's mouth turned down in an ugly line. "All I care to know."

Maurie's heart was suddenly racing. "Please, tell me what you know. Anything."

Maurie's anguished plea caused the woman's expression to soften. "'Tain't my place to be saying nothing. But you'd be doing yourself a favor to quit digging around things best left dead and buried. And don't be bothering Father Sashoney. He's got better things to do than concern himself with the likes of Maelene O'Mallory." With that she shut the door.

Maurie called after her, but when a long moment of waiting passed, Maurie ` 1ew the woman wasn't going to open the door again.

All the way back to the boardinghouse, tears of frustration and anger were moist on her cheeks. Why had the woman used that tone of voice when she referred to "the likes of Maelene O'Mallory"? And why had she shut the door in her face, refusing to talk to her? Maurie's chest was filled with an ache that had nothing to do with the labored pedaling of the old bike.

I can handle this, she lectured herself. Whatever she found out about her mother would not change the way she felt about herself. *I know who I am.* But the valiant declaration rang hollow—she'd never been much good at lying to herself. All right, face the truth. She had come to Ireland to search for her parentage, but Father Sashoney, Daylan and the housekeeper had reacted the same way when she mentioned Maelene O'Mallory. They had warned her about stirring up the past. What if the facts of her heritage turned out to be the destructive kind? What then? What would be served? Her life with her adoptive parents had been a happy one. Why not go back home and live in blissful ignorance of a heritage that she could not change anyway? The answer was simple.

Because I can't.

Mrs. Duffy had just finished collecting the offering of a dozen clucking hens when Maurie rode into the yard and parked the bike at the back gate. Carrying a basketful of speckled eggs, the landlady walked back to the house with Maurie. "Well, now, you've got some color in your cheeks. Where'd you pedal to this mornin'?"

"To the church to talk to Father Sashoney. But he wasn't there."

Mrs. Duffy frowned as she placed the basket on the kitchen table. "I guess my memory is failing me. I was thinking you said you weren't Catholic."

"I'm not. I wanted to ask him some questions."

"Oh, of course. The college paper you're doing. What is it exactly ye be writing about? Would you be liking another cup of coffee while I get some bean soup simmering for lunch?"

"If I'm not in the way..."

"Just set yourself down." She eyed Maurie frankly as she poured the coffee. "Ye be looking like someone who's a mite homesick. Happens that way sometimes. Ireland's not like any other country. 'Tis a land of moods. Some folks say it holds a terrible beauty." She gave Maurie a knowing nod. "And sometimes it touches the soul darkly."

Maurie fought an urge to pour out everything. Tell the motherly woman about her horrible nightmares, the frightening tailspin her feelings for Daylan had taken and the ominous feeling that something dark and sinister was reaching out to her from her mother's grave. But what good would it do to dump her emotional anxieties on Mrs. Duffy? The landlady would probably view her as just a neurotic American and be uneasy in her presence. As Maurie watched the kindly, practical woman bustle happily around her kitchen, the impulse to pour out her confusion died.

All right, then. *Find the answers yourself.* Maurie put down her coffee mug. "I've just begun work on my independent study," she lied, smiling at Mrs. Duffy. "I wanted to ask Father Sashoney about a Maelene O'Mallory."

Mrs. Duffy stopped sorting rocks from a pile of beans. "Maelene O'Mallory? Faith, it's been a long time since I heard that name. Why on earth are you asking about her?"

Maurie shrugged as if there wasn't any real reason. "I just happened upon her grave yesterday. Old cemeteries hold a fascination for me," she said honestly. "I'm always poking around some of the old burial grounds we have in New England. You can learn a lot about social customs from some of the tombstones."

"Och, I suppose you can," Mrs. Duffy said, but her lips were pursed as if cemeteries had one use only—to let the people buried there rest in peace. Her forehead furrowed as she locked eyes with Maurie. "Sure and I don't want anyone traipsing around my grave, asking questions about me that are none of their business."

It is my business, Maurie railed silently. What if she told the landlady that Maelene O'Mallory was her mother? The woman would probably clam up the way the priest and his housekeeper had. Better to act like a curious tourist, she thought. "I went to the cemetery yesterday because Father Sashoney had said I might be interested in the site of an old Catholic home and orphanage." *Almost the truth.*

"Don't know why anybody would want to spend time in that unhappy place. Let the poor souls rest in peace, I say."

"So many of the buried were women my own age," offered Maurie. "I guess I was taken by the name Maelene—and the idea of someone dying so young." Maurie tried to keep her voice casual. "I couldn't help but wonder about the tragic circumstances that led her to that lonely grave. Do you know anything about her?''

''No more than anybody else,'' she said flatly. ''I never had anything to do with the home or orphanage. But any girl connected with Jake Flintery got her name battered about—and none to the good, either.''

Maurie's mouth went suddenly dry. She swallowed hard. ''Jake Flintery?''

''A lawless renegade of the first water. Led a band of so-called patriots in the early 1960s. Had a secret society, they did. Killed a half-dozen estate owners and were responsible for blowing up a train that killed a lot of innocent people. They called themselves the Avengers. Jack Flintery took a liking to an orphaned young woman. Maelene O'Mallory, so the story goes.''

''You mean . . . she was his sweetheart?''

''When Flintery saw a woman he wanted, he took her, willing or not. Some say he picked on the wrong girl.''

''Why? What happened?''

''No one really knows. Jake's body was found battered and broken on some rocks at the foot of a cliff. No telling who shoved him to his death, but the money was on Maelene. She went to the home shortly after that—gave birth and died there.''

The room whirled in a sickening fashion. Maurie gripped the table with her sweaty hands. *A terrorist father and a murderess mother.* No wonder everyone looked at her strangely when she talked about Mae-lene O'Mallory. She had been warned to leave the past alone, and now it was too late. The ugly story was her heritage.

"Are you feeling all right, girl?" asked Mrs. Duffy, noticing the beads of sweat forming at Maurie's fore-head.

Maurie stared at her for a moment and then she stammered, "I...I think...I'll go upstairs and lie down."

"Good idea. Maybe you shouldn't have been exer-cising so much. The church is a far piece from here for someone not used to cycling. And with you not hav-ing a good night and all. Maybe you should crawl un-der the covers and take yourself a good sleep."

And perhaps to dream? Maurie nodded, but she knew that she couldn't let herself be drawn into that other frightening existence. Not now. Not when her head was reeling with emotions that stabbed the mid-dle of her stomach painfully. What a mockery of her enthusiastic pilgrimage to the land of her birth!

"I'm fixing bean-and-ham soup for lunch," prom-ised Mrs. Duffy as Maurie left the kitchen.

Hysterical laughter bubbled up in her throat as she climbed the stairs to her room. *Seek and ye shall find.* Mrs. Duffy's story had identified her father. And the only unknown fact about her mother was whether or not she had been the one who shoved him over the cliff to his death.

Maurie closed the door to her room and locked it, a futile gesture to keep out the ugly world that had engulfed her with every word from Mrs. Duffy's mouth.

Sitting on the edge of the bed, she stared at a worn braided rug without seeing the myriad patterns and colors. A nausea in her stomach brought bitter bile into her mouth.

There had to be some mistake. Two women named Maelene O'Mallory. Two women who had gone to the home to give birth. Two women who—

Stop it! With a force of will she stopped the hysterical churning of her thoughts. She straightened her back and stiffened against the truth. There had been only one Maelene O'Mallory. And the letter from Father Flynn to her adoptive parents had named that person as her birth mother. And now she knew her father. A despicable terrorist, Jake Flintery.

A quiet knock on her door jerked her head around. "Maurie, are you awake?"

Daylan. She stared at the locked door, smothering her breath in her throat. *He had known.* When she told him the name of her mother that first night in the car, he had looked at her strangely—and now she knew why. He knew about her mother and Jake Flintery. Maybe that's why he'd been so furious when he saw her spying on him. He remembered whose blood ran in her veins.

She heard his footsteps fading away. Her eyes stung with hot tears, a mixture of anger and despair. She hated him for deceiving her, for letting her believe that he knew nothing about her background. And all the time he must have known the sordid details of her birth.

She put her head down on her pillow, closed her eyes and let the tears flow. Why had she ever come to this horrible place? Why hadn't she been satisfied to accept the wonderful upbringing her adoptive parents had given her? Her well-ordered life had been fulfilling. There had been disappointments in her relationships with men, but nothing like the devastation she felt when thinking about Daylan O'Shane. How ironic it was. She had expected to enrich her life by searching for her Irish roots, not destroy it!

She forgot to guard herself against falling asleep. A blessed weariness eased her into a deep and restful nap. When a knocking at her door awoke her an hour later, she started with a jerk. She had been asleep. *But no dreams.*

"Maurie, I've brought up a bit o' lunch," called Mrs. Duffy. "It's past two o'clock and you really should eat something."

Maurie sped to the door. "How thoughtful of you. I guess I slept through lunch. And I do feel hungry," she said with a note of surprise. The nap had done wonders to mend the devastation she'd felt earlier.

"I'm glad to see you're feeling better. Sure and I thought you might be comin' down with something." She set the tray on a small table beside the bed. "We can't have you missing meals and feeling poorly. Mr. O'Shane was asking about you. I told him you'd gone to your room to rest. I promised to keep an eye on you. Come on, now, have yourself some soup and salad. I even buttered a slice of brown stone-ground bread for you. Stick to your ribs, it will."

She waited until Maurie had taken a couple of bites of the bread before she started toward the door. Then she stopped and wrinkled her forehead. "It's funny you should be asking about Maelene O'Mallory. I remember now that Tansie said something about her the other day."

Maurie put down the bread. The bite in her mouth was suddenly large and dry. "What did she say about her?"

"I don't rightly remember. But you could ask Tansie, if you've a mind too. She's the one to answer your questions all right. She probably knows all there is to know."

"Why?"

"Because some twenty-odd years ago, Tansie was a young postulant at the Catholic home when Maelene O'Mallory was there. That was before Tansie was tossed out of the order for practicing witchcraft."

CHAPTER EIGHT

Lowering clouds made the fields and woods resemble a wet-wash painting as Maurie headed down the twisting path that Mrs. Duffy had said led to Tansie's small cottage less than a mile away. A heaviness in the air warned of impending rain, and Maurie quickened her steps. A frenzied urgency fueled her body. *Tansie had known her mother.* A thousand questions whirled in her mind like dry leaves driven by a devil's wind. She was scarcely aware of a hovering silence as green-black trees closed in around her.

As she plunged deeper into a coppice of willow and hawthorn trees, decaying wood and soggy earth created a dank fecund smell, and only feeble spears of sunlight pierced a thick canopy of branches overhead. Green moss clinging to tree trunks shone wetly against the blackish bark, and her footsteps left imprints in the soggy deadfall as she hurried forward.

"Stay on the path," the landlady had warned her. "You don't want to be wandering off into the nearby bog. 'Tis a mystery to me why you'd be wanting to start out this very minute when you've been feeling so poorly. Sorry I am that I mentioned Tansie's name.

Time enough to talk with her when the sun's a shinin'.''

Maurie had made some vague reply. She didn't want to tell Mrs. Duffy that her mother had been Maelene O'Mallory, which was foolish. It was only a matter of time before the kindly lady would learn that her new boarder was the illegitimate child of the infamous Jake Flintery.

She hugged herself as she walked through the woods. The air held a chill that penetrated her clothing and lay wetly on her skin. A hushed waiting silence was like brooding unseen watchers lurking behind every tree and crusted rock. Like an intruder in a secret place, her footsteps heralded her passage through a tunnel of twisted trees.

She almost turned back several times as a feeling that she might never emerge from the never-ending dark woods brought a nervous fluttering to her chest. No wonder the Irish were filled with dark superstitions, she thought, glancing around. Shadows flickered in such a way as to create the impression of fey creatures lurking on every side of the path. Was she alone? Or was there a host of eyes watching her?

She forced herself to concentrate on the purpose of her visit. Tansie would verify what she already knew. As painful as it might be, she wanted to know all the facts.

I'll have to leave Glenmara soon, she thought, before people begin pointing me out in the street. There was no way to keep her identity a secret, not with the gossip grapevine emerging from Mrs. Duffy's very kitchen. And if Ireland was anything like the States, the news media would descend on her like vultures, resurrecting the villainous exploits of her father and branding her with them. No, she wouldn't put herself through that. She'd leave after she learned as much as she could about her mother. As painful as it might be, she wanted to hear all the stories about Maelene and the notorious terrorist who had been her father.

Even though she had kept her eyes on the path, her swimming thoughts had clouded her attention. She stopped suddenly, blinking, as a pile of rocks rose up in front of her, blocking her way.

Where was the path?

She turned around.

Panic began to rise in her chest. She was surrounded by an infinity of dark tree trunks. No matter which direction she turned, her path was blocked.

Trees and rocks crowded in on her from every direction. Clinging black vines reached out for her as she bolted through dense undergrowth.

Stay on the path. You don't want to be wandering off into the nearby bog.

Maurie froze. Afraid to move. A thrashing in some branches above her jerked her eyes up to the crown of a hawthorn tree. A shiny black crow sat there looking down at her. It gave a loud caw, spread its ebony wings and flew to a tree just ahead of her. Looking at her with beady eyes, the bird waited, then flew ahead to another tree. Each time it waited as Maurie slowly followed the crow's passage through the trees.

Maurie smelled smoke from a peat fire before she saw the house crouched darkly in a sunken enclosure ringed by gray rocks. Dark woody vines covered the exterior walls, and a steep thatched roof was topped by a rock chimney. A narrow front door was open and Tansie stood there watching.

"Lost your way, did ye?" she asked with a faint tucking of a smile at the corner of her mouth.

Maurie looked up at the black bird perched on a ledge above the door. Then her eyes fell to Tansie's wizened face. "The crow showed me the way."

Tansie nodded as if there were nothing remarkable about that. "Come in. I've been expecting you."

There was no way she could have known I was coming. I didn't know it myself.

Maurie entered the one-room dwelling. In a reflex action, she ducked, thinking that cobwebs were hanging from the ceiling. When her eyes adjusted to the dim light, she realized with relief that an array of dried plants were suspended from the ceiling rafters. A mingling of aromas from herbs and oils lay heavy in the air, and Maurie put her hand on the back of an old chair to steady herself as a dizziness overtook her. She found it hard to breathe, and she sat quickly in a chair by a crude table.

A gray cat with bright yellow eyes looked down at her from a mantel above a fireplace, holding her with a mesmerizing stare. Then he stretched on stiff legs and with a light spring landed on the dirt floor beside her.

She stiffened as the animal began threading through her legs. The warmth of its furry body came through the denim cloth of her jeans. With a deliberate arching of his back, the cat massaged her legs. Caress. Purr. Caress. Purr. The tension in Maurie's body eased away.

"That's enough, Belaud," Tansie said to the cat with a wave of her hand. The animal bounded back on the mantel and settled into its staring position.

Tansie put two crudely shaped cups and a teapot on the table in front of Maurie. As if it was the most ordinary of tea parties, the wizened little woman poured a steamy hot liquid into the chipped cups and offered one to Maurie.

She took the cup but hesitated to sip the strange brew. The color was an unusual green and the aroma was unfamiliar. Steam rose from the peculiar liquid as she stared at it, wondering if the tea was made from ingredients as eerie as everything else about this bizarre woman.

Sitting on a high stool, Tansie dominated the table, diminishing Maurie's own five feet, seven inches. As the woman looked down at her, she exuded an aura of command.

"The tea is not to your liking?" Tansie asked, as Maurie continued to hold the cup between her hands without raising it to her lips. "'Tis a blend of rare herbs hidden from the eye and only plucked by those with dark vision. A special brew—just for you. Drink."

Maurie took a sip and found the liquid's taste robust but pleasant. With every sip the urgency and anxiety she had felt earlier disappeared. Her dizziness passed and a strange lassitude remained in her legs from the cat's furry massage. Imperceptibly she slipped into a different plain of awareness, one that seemed suspended from the past, the future and even the present.

Tansie waited until Maurie had finished the first cup. As she poured a second, she asked, "And why have ye come?" Her voice was like the whisper of wind through soft leaves.

Maurie set down her cup. She searched through the fuzzy layers that coated her thoughts. "My mother..." she said haltingly. "I came to find my mother."

"But ye found her," responded Tansie in that same soothing tone. "On the hill. In her grave. Remember? I saw ye there."

Maurie nodded. "Yes. You frightened me when I thought I was alone at the ruins." Her thoughts were slow and sluggish. "Why did you follow me?"

"'Twas ye who followed me."

Maurie put a hand up to her head as if to clear it. "No. Father Sashoney told me about the cemetery. I went there because..." she began, the reason skidding away from her as her mind reached for it. "Because..."

"Because ye sought the place where ye drew your first breath of life. There, on that windy knoll, in the early light of morning, ye lifted yer first wail to the heavens."

"And you were there—with my mother."

Tansie's blue eyes were like the center glow of a coal fire and shone out of her withered face with blinding intensity. Maurie raised a hand to shield her eyes from the piercing assault of the woman's gaze.

"Ye might find yer own way to the past," she said.

"I can't. You have to help me."

"I can do no more but lead you through the web of dreams."

We sleep and then we die. Maurie's head was beginning to ache. Dreams. Dreams. *We are such stuff as dreams are made on, and our little life is rounded with a sleep.* The quotation lurched into the front of her mind with the clang of a bell.

"Ye must go now," Tansie said. "Someone is coming for ye."

Maurie opened her mouth to protest, but the words died in her throat. A horse's neigh, heavy footsteps and a pounding on the door shattered the tranquility of the shadowy room.

Daylan called her name. "Maurie! Maurie, are you in there?"

Tansie slipped off her stool and retreated into the shadows, utterly ignoring the intrusion. Maurie crossed the room and opened the door. He stood there, shocks of moist hair falling forward and the corners of his dark eyes creased with worry.

"I couldn't believe it when Mrs. Duffy told me you'd set off by yourself to find this godforsaken place," he lashed out. "There are treacherous bogs ready to suck you under if you'd gotten lost."

She nodded as her head began to clear in the fresh air. Had she been hopelessly lost until a black crow had led her to Tansie's doorstep? Everything seemed preposterous—the crow, the weird tea party and even the idea that Tansie had been present at her birth.

Maurie's confusion must have been evident in her expression, for he softened his tone. "Mrs. Duffy said you'd been feeling poorly, Maurie. Why in God's good name would you get out of bed and take the risk of getting lost when a storm's coming up?"

"I...I..." she stammered. "I came for answers about my mother."

"Surely you don't believe that stuff about Tansie possessing magical powers? She's got a racket going, just like all fortune-tellers who'll tell you what you want to know for money in their hands. I would have thought you above giving any credence to such nonsense." He made an impatient wave with his hand. "I borrowed a horse to bring you back. Come on, let's get out of here before the storm hits.''

Maurie gave a hasty glance through the door into the darkened room. Only the cat's unblinking yellow eyes shone clearly in the shadows. She couldn't see Tansie at all, and suddenly Maurie felt confused, lost. A shiver shook her shoulders.

''It's all right,'' he soothed. ''I'll have you safely back in no time.'' He put an arm around her and led her to his tethered horse.

He gave her a boost into the saddle, and she was glad she'd worn walking boots that fit into the stirrups. He swung up onto the rump of the sorrel horse, behind Maurie. With an arm on each side of her, he held the reins and gave the horse a light kick with his heels. The animal trotted off in the opposite direction from the wooded path she had followed earlier.

Daylan guided the horse up a steep rocky slope littered with rocks and tufts of grass. Once they reached the crest, they rode along the top of the rolling hill.

Maurie held on to the saddle horn as the horse's movements sent her swaying from side to side. She leaned back against Daylan to keep her balance, and he tightened his arms and leaned his face close to hers. His warm breath bathed her neck, and once his lips touched her cheek in a fleeting kiss that sent a tingling sensation spiraling through her. Her thoughts were still in a peculiar state of suspension, and she found herself smiling to herself. Her feeling of confusion was gone. She felt safe. Protected.

They reached a rutted road just as the first raindrop touched her head and the sound of rumbling thunder was like approaching artillery. Daylan swore and kicked the horse into a full gallop. The wind whipped Maurie's face and tossed her hair. An exhilaration like madness swept through her. She wanted to laugh and shout, give herself up to the bewildering sensation of utter joy. Every sensory bud in her body was alive with heightened awareness. She was totally alive—perhaps for the first time in her life.

The powerful stride of the horse sent the ground racing beneath her, and she felt the flow of the animal's muscular strength surging into her own body. The galloping horse was like a meteor shooting across the sky. She wanted the magical moment to go on forever, but over the next rise, the boardinghouse appeared below them. The horse gave an extra spurt of speed and they reached the clearing behind the house just before the lowering heavens gave up their cache of rain.

Daylan slipped from the horse's back, then led the animal into the old stone barn. He swung the large door shut just as the rain began to come down in torrents on the barn's steep roof.

"Made it just in time," he said with satisfaction. As he looped the reins over a post, Maurie jumped down from the saddle before he could offer a hand. She stood back as he quickly unfastened the cinch and swung the saddle off the horse's back.

She watched as he threw a blanket over the animal and then began to rub down the glistening reddish hide. His strokes moved gracefully over the horse's shoulders, thighs, lower legs and rump. As Maurie watched Daylan, a warm stirring of sexual desire crept through her. Every movement of his body was a tantalizing promise of his commanding masculinity. As his dexterous hands traced the warm contours of the horse's body, she felt his gentle strokes on her own skin. She had never felt that kind of desire. An aching need that rose full-blown and demanding brought beads of perspiration to her brow.

She should leave. Walk out the door. Let the rain pour over her. Cool the physical desire sluicing hotly through her. It was insanity to want this man so passionately. An exhilarating, all-consuming kind of madness.

Outside the storm raged with thunder and lightning while cascades of water poured off the roof and down the stone walls. But inside the old barn, there was a waiting stillness. A charged atmosphere.

Daylan put the horse in a stall. Filled a water bucket and added some feed to a small trough. And all the time, she watched. After he closed the stall door, he turned around slowly. His eyes searched hers. For a long moment neither moved, and yet in some strange way they were already in the throes of lovemaking.

Her breathing was shallow. A groan sounded deep in his chest. The air was charged with mounting desire.

He drew her against the demanding tenseness of his body, and his mouth found hers with a possessive capture that allowed no escape. He parted her lips and his questing tongue brought a fiery arousal within her. This was desire as she had never known it, a passion that blotted out all thinking and a hunger that refused to be appeased.

With the ease of lifting a child in his arms, he swept her up and carried her to a corner of the barn where hired help had made a pallet of canvas and blankets. As their clothes fell away, they lay pressed together with only the dim light of the barn concealing their nakedness. His hands found the soft fullness of her breasts and she felt sweet pain as his mouth captured a hardening nipple.

Brushing back the moist hair drifting forward on her cheeks, he whispered, "'Tis the beauty of shimmering emeralds in her eyes, and the sweet softness of a misty morn upon her skin."

The lilt of his Irish brogue gave a musical cadence to his murmurings. He buried his face in the silky cleft of her breasts and then let his lips trail down her body to the softness of her thighs. She whimpered as she buried her head against his chest and her arms circled his body. He responded to her urging, and as he slipped inside her, she received him with an explosive cry.

She had never experienced pure fulfillment before and it left her weak, gasping his name.

Their passion spent, he rolled to one side, holding her tightly. She lay quietly in his arms, her head resting on his chest. Tears crowded into the corner of her eyes and began flowing down her cheeks. Now she knew what love was, an all-consuming giving of oneself wholly, completely, on every level of one's being. No holding back. The knowledge frightened her.

Seeing her wet cheeks, he touched the warm tears with a fingertip, asking quietly, "Disappointed?"

She smiled her answer.

"But unhappy...because we've made love?"

She shook her head. "No, not that, either."

"Then what?"

"I guess I don't like feeling vulnerable. It frightens me. Feeling this way frightens me."

"Why?" he asked quietly, as he leaned over her. His naked body was so utterly seductive and inviting that Maurie felt desire beginning to build again.

"Because there's something about you that... that..." She searched for the right word. "That I don't trust."

His lips curved in a slight smile. "Well, after what's just happened, I can't say that you should."

"I don't mean that. We both know there was no reluctance on my part." She gave him a wry smile. "In fact, I don't know who seduced whom." She slipped away from him and reached for the clothes hastily tossed in a heap.

"It's still raining. Why the hurry?" He reached up and tried to pull her back down beside him.

"No. Please . . . can't we . . . talk?"

"And why would ye be wanting to talk—when there's still coals burning hotly in passion's fire?"

It took all the willpower she could muster not to give in to the mesmerizing persuasion in his voice and touch. She slipped into her clothes before she turned to face him. "When I told you my mother's name, you never let on that you'd heard it before. Why?" she demanded.

"So you found out," he said sadly. "I knew it was only a matter of time."

"So you lied to me?"

"I didn't lie. I just kept my silence. I knew how you'd react."

She bristled. "And how should I react to hearing such a sordid tale about my beginnings? My father was a terrorist and my mother guilty of shoving him off a cliff to his death."

"You don't know how much is the truth and how much is embellishment," he cautioned.

"I know my mother was Maelene O'Mallory. Her lover was Jake Flintery, a leader of the Avengers, who blew up a train that killed many innocent people. Right? And I shouldn't let the fact that the blood of this despicable killer runs in my veins bother me in the least?'' Her lower lip trembled. ''How could my mother have had anything to do with a man like that?''

''Don't be so hard on someone you didn't know.''

''If what they say about him is true, Jake Flintery was a killer.''

''There are always two sides to violence. Maybe Jake couldn't see any other way to try and right the injustices he saw around him. Ireland has many festering hatreds. And open wounds that refuse to heal.'' His face was suddenly void of softness. His tone was hard and held an edge of bitterness.

''I don't see how she could have closed her eyes to the horrible things he did.''

''Don't judge your mother harshly because she loved a man everyone else hated. Sometimes there is no choice.''

''There's always a choice,'' she said stubbornly.

He shook his head sadly. ''Love cannot be ruled.''

Maurie stared at him with a quivering of fear in her stomach. *Love cannot be ruled.* Was there an ominous truth in the words? A warning? Was he trying to tell her she was guilty of loving the same kind of man who had brought disaster upon her mother?

CHAPTER NINE

All through dinner Maurie pushed around bits of food on her plate. Caught in an emotional and mental fog, she didn't taste anything she was eating and failed to hear when someone spoke to her. Every nerve seemed to flare with an all-consuming awareness of the man sitting across from her. Even when she was not looking at Daylan and deliberately kept her gaze fixed on her plate, she was aware of every breath he drew, every movement he made as he turned to speak to Mrs. Duffy and the Moreheads. His deep voice brought back the memory of whispered endearments, and a glimpse of his hands on the table triggered remembered caresses.

"Are you sure you've not caught a chill?" asked Mrs. Duffy, eyeing Maurie's plate. "You've hardly touched your food."

Maurie managed a reassuring smile. "Everything is delicious," she said hastily, wanting to ease the frown from her landlady's face. "Quite different from what I'm used to. I'm afraid my usual fare is quick packaged dinners that taste like cardboard."

"It's good wholesome food you're needing to put some meat on them bones," she stated flatly.

"And a nice set of bones they are," Daylan said, with a teasing glint in his eyes.

"She needs to put on twenty pounds," Mrs. Duffy insisted.

Mrs. Morehead nodded in agreement as she reached out dimpled arms for another slice of meat pie.

"You're not much of a cook then, Miss Miller?" asked Daylan, a teasing lilt to his voice. The use of her surname mocked the charge of electricity that forked between them as their eyes met.

"The kitchen is not my favorite room in the house," she answered evenly, hoping that the warm flush she felt wasn't creeping into her cheeks.

Mrs. Morehead picked up the conversation, talking about a new patio room she and her husband had just added to their house, but her voice was no more than the faint whine of an insect in Maurie's consciousness.

As Maurie looked across the table at Daylan, nothing had meaning except the fierce hunger mounting in the lovemaking they carried on with their eyes. A naked desire shut out everything and everyone. She was locked in his wordless embrace when Mrs. Duffy repeated her name in an impatient tone and asked her something.

Maurie blinked. The invisible chord that tied her to Daylan's gaze snapped. For a moment, the room spun. She felt weak, almost ill.

"Did you enjoy your visit with Tansie?"

The question was so unexpected that for a moment Maurie just stared at Mrs. Duffy without answering. Her visit to the odd woman's house had been overshadowed by the unleashed passion between her and Daylan.

Mrs. Duffy's pink forehead puckered. "Isn't that where you went this afternoon?"

"Yes, that's where I found her," Daylan answered for her. "Thanks for the loan of your horse. We would have been caught in a downpour without it."

"Did you have any trouble finding the place, Maurie? I became a little worried about your wandering off the path. Dangerous bogs lie hidden in those thick drifts of trees. I'm glad you didn't get lost."

"No, I found it without any trouble," she lied. The memory of the black crow leading the way through the thick coppice was vivid. She had been totally lost until the bird had come to her rescue, flapping its wings and cawing as she followed it to the doorstep of the obscure little house. After that her memories became less sharp. She couldn't recall clearly what had taken place in the dark cottage except that she'd enjoyed some strange-tasting tea.

"I hope Tansie didn't frighten you none. She's a strange one. Goes her own way, she does. Always has.'' Mrs. Duffy gave a dismissing wave of her hand. ''Pshaw, I've never believed half the stories passed around about her.''

''What stories?'' asked Maurie, her throat suddenly tight.

''Sure and Tansie has a special 'sight' about some things.''

A bit of tansy for your dreams. On more than one occasion the bizarre woman seemed to know that she had been drawn into the recurring dream where she became Dawna. But how could that be? A dream didn't belong to anyone but the dreamer—*unless it wasn't really a dream.*

''I'll never be believing she's a black witch,'' offered Mrs. Duffy. ''In league with the devil, they said. That's why she was dismissed from the order, you know. Accused of practicing witchcraft.''

Mrs. Morehead tittered. ''A black witch? How exciting. Does she weave spells?''

Maurie couldn't breathe. *Does she weave spells?* From the moment the spray of tansy flowers had been thrust into her hand, she had felt herself caught in a mesh of the woman's weaving. She had tried to dismiss everything that had happened as having a logical explanation, but a sickening certainty that there was no rational basis for the horrid dreams made her lash out defiantly. ''No, I don't believe it. Tansie's odd— but she's not a witch.''

"You can't deny there are dark spirits among us," Mrs. Duffy countered. "I myself have heard the wail of a banshee coming to collect the dead. I was sitting by my mother's dying side, and before my very eyes I saw the shadow of a horrible hag with a wrinkled face and distorted features holding her outstretched arms toward the bed. I cried and covered my face. When I looked again, the banshee was gone—and my mother was dead."

Mrs. Morehead gave a nervous laugh. "All this talk of witches and banshees makes for good ghost stories."

"Just a bunch of superstitious nonsense if you ask me," Mr. Morehead replied in his blunt way.

"Then you don't believe in the Prince of Darkness?" Daylan challenged. "Some say he walks among us, leading the innocent down the paths of evil." His smile was condescending.

Maurie stared at him. This was the man whom a moment ago she had desired with unbridled passion. An unreadable glint like blue fire glowed in the depths of his dark eyes. The intensity of his expression shut off the air to Maurie's chest. She suddenly felt like someone drowning, drawn deeper and deeper into a suffocating helplessness.

After dinner, Daylan told her he was sorry but he had to go out for a while. "See you in the morning, Maurie," he whispered gently as they stood together in the front hall. "Sweet dreams." He touched a kiss to her hairline.

On one level, she yearned to lean into him and feel the powerful surge of his strength as he drew her to him. She wanted him to fill her mind with the same kind of blinding euphoria that had overtaken her when he'd made love to her. And on another level she was strangely relieved, as if for the moment, she had been allowed to regain possession of herself.

After he'd gone, she sat in the small living room until bedtime, staring at a book without seeing the words and listening in a detached fashion to the Moreheads and Mrs. Duffy. She felt off balance, as if a part of herself was missing. Where did Daylan go at night? Maybe he was married. A wife with kids. Or maybe he had another sweetheart. Someone who curled up with him and felt his body heat surging— *Stop it!* She was a fool to torture herself this way.

She forced herself to listen to the Moreheads as they planned the next leg of their trip. This would be their last night in Glenmara.

Their last night. What if she followed their lead and left tomorrow? She doubted if she could get an immediate flight home, but she could play tourist for a day or two, take a bus tour and escape to a different part of Ireland. *Escape.* That was the right word. She felt trapped. A prisoner of some kind. *What utter nonsense,* she scolded herself. Where was her usual matter-of-fact, common-sense approach to life? If anything, she'd always been too pragmatic, too down-to-earth to let her feelings get away from her. She had never let any man send her reeling with a look or soft word, but now her impatience with "fools in love" came back to haunt her as a mounting hunger filled her body. She couldn't leave. An insatiable greed had overtaken her. She had no power against it. She had to have Daylan's arms around her, his lean strong body possessing hers. Maybe it was love, and maybe it was something else.

Maurie said good-night to the others and went upstairs to her room. The events of the day whirled in her mind as she stood at her bedroom window, her body alive and tingling. A restless frustration drove away all semblance of sleep. The rainstorm had passed over, but the heavens were still dark, with heavy clouds blanketing the moon. She leaned her forehead against the cool pane of the glass, closed her eyes against the warring emotions that rose and fell like a restless surf.

After a few minutes she closed the curtains and crossed the hall to the bathroom. She filled the old-fashioned, claw-footed tub with hot water and then lay immersed to her chin, the warmth of the water easing away her tension. As she bathed with the sweet lavender-scented soap, the same lassitude she'd felt from the rubbing of Tansie's cat enveloped her.

After her bath she padded back to her room, slipped into bed and stretched out with a sigh of content-ment. Tomorrow was soon enough to sort out the devastating and conflicting happenings of today. Tomorrow she would pursue information about her parentage. She might even go back to Tansie to ask the questions that still remained unanswered. Tomorrow would be time enough to confront her feelings about Daylan. Tomorrow...

On the edge of sleep, she heard the soft opening of her door. A small band of light sliced across the room and she saw his silhouetted figure in the doorway. *He had come to her.* A rush of joy quickened her breath. The aching hunger she had suppressed now leapt through her with unleashed fury. Her pulse fluttered wildly. She was glad her skin smelled of lavender and her hair lay shiny clean around her face. They would have all the hours of the night for making love.

"Daylan," she murmured in a passion-cloaked voice as he stood beside her bed. She held out her arms to him.

"You bitch!"

He grabbed her by the shoulders and his fingernails bit harshly into her soft flesh. "I ought to kill you and be done with it!"

She opened her mouth to cry out, but he clapped his hand over her mouth. "No, Dawna. No screaming. You need to be taught a lesson."

Maurie bit into the flesh of his palm.

He jerked his hand away. He swore, his teeth shining white above the dark line of his mustache. He reached for her and she lunged across the wide bed. He grabbed her back. She scrambled to free herself from the confining bedclothes.

She had one foot on the soft rug beside the bed when she felt the blow on the back of her head. She fell forward and hit the floor, striking her cheek.

''No, no,'' she whimpered. She lay there, unable to move. Her breath caught in her throat. Her stomach fluttered with the whipping of a thousand frantic wings.

Oliver. She had to get away from Oliver.

Her frantic gaze swept upward. The huge bed with its luxurious covers had disappeared. Oliver was gone.

She was lying on the floor beside her narrow bed, and her fingers were dug into the braids of Mrs. Duffy's rug. The only sounds were her strangled breathing and a whimpering sob that caught in her throat.

CHAPTER TEN

Maurie stayed awake the rest of the night. She sat up against the headboard, her back rigid and every muscle guarded against her drifting off to sleep again. A cold perspiration coated her skin as the terror of the nightmare stayed with her. Her head reeled dizzily and she was confused. At what point had the nightmare begun? Frowning, she tried to remember. She had been fantasizing about Daylan. The door had opened and the man she'd thought was him had come to her. She'd held out her arms to welcome him to her bed. Then everything had changed. The man standing by her bed was not Daylan. He called her Dawna, and the lover she had eagerly welcomed was the cruel, sadistic Oliver.

Why? Why was her subconscious tormenting her? Why were the two men, Daylan and Oliver, so much alike in her mind and yet so different? *Unless they were two parts of the same man?*

But how could that be?

She put a hand against her forehead as she winced against the headache that began to thump behind her eyes. I must be losing my mind, she thought. She wasn't sure anymore which images in her mind were real. Was the borderline between rational fears and imagined ones becoming imperceptible?

Is this the beginning of madness?

The constant uncertainty and the fear that the nightmare would engulf her and catch her unawares was present with every breath she drew. Time ticked by slowly. She clutched the homemade quilt defiantly as if to forestall its change into the silken cover of her nightmare. In a moment of rising panic, she pinched her arm. The pain was reassuring. *I'm awake.*

When the first pearly gray of dawn touched her window, lining the edges of the curtains, she eased her stiff legs over the side of the bed. She sat there for a moment, looking down at the braided rug. Thank God, she had fallen out of bed and been rudely awakened from the nightmare. What would have happened to her as Dawna if the dream had continued?

I ought to kill you and be done with it. Oliver's voice rang in her ears.

A chill crept up her spine. No one could be murdered in a dream.

Could they?

There were no sounds in the house when she was ready to go downstairs. As she left her room, she glanced down the hall at Daylan's closed door. He had not come back, she was sure of it. There had been no quiet footsteps in the hall all night long. What would keep a man bartering in homemade lace out all night?

A good question, she thought. One that invited all kinds of bewildering answers. One thing was certain. The business that took him away at night had nothing to do with cottage industry. He had glibly spun the tale about meeting with unscrupulous men who were trying to control the lace makers in the area, and she was certain he had lied to her about his reason for being in Glenmara.

And what other lies had he told her? she asked herself. Had he gone from her arms to another besotted sweetheart? What did she really know about Daylan O'Shane? Nothing. Absolutely nothing. She was falling in love with a phantom stranger.

A deep weariness overtook her. Shadows under her eyes betrayed her sleepless night, and lines around her mouth were stiff and tense. She hugged herself as she went down the stairs, shivering in her knit sweater and black stretch pants. What's happening to me? Have I caught some kind of a mysterious virus? She prayed it was so. God knows she'd welcome a physical ailment that could be cured with a round of pills and chicken soup.

Maurie had already consumed one cup of coffee by the time Mrs. Duffy came downstairs. The landlady saw her sitting at the table, hunched over her coffee mug with her head propped on one hand. Her eyes were heavy and her gaze blurry from sleeplessness.

"God love us," the woman said by way of greeting. "You look like death warmed over. The rooster hasn't even crowed yet. Faith, I'm up a half hour early 'cause this is market day."

There was a slight accusing edge in the woman's tone, as if she wasn't about to brook any extra landlady responsibilities on such a busy day.

"I couldn't sleep." Maurie offered the explanation without elaboration since Mrs. Duffy's briskness didn't invite any confidences. The truth that she had lain awake all night, terrified of going to sleep, would have only puzzled the practical widow. She'd have dismissed it as utter nonsense. And considering the strangeness of the situation, Maurie wouldn't have blamed her.

Spry and energetic, Mrs. Duffy bustled around the room and Maurie's frayed nerves began to knit as she watched her. She offered to help and was grateful that the landlady accepted. She set the dining room table, and soon the kitchen was filled with the odors of frying bacon, fresh-baked biscuits and salted kippers. The aura of normalcy did wonders for putting Maurie's phantoms of the night at bay.

When Daylan didn't show up for breakfast, the Moreheads expressed their disappointment at not having a chance to tell him goodbye.

"Such a nice young man," Mrs. Morehead said with a slight blush rising in her cheeks. Daylan's flattering attention had left a pleasant remembrance. The English couple were busily making ready to continue their trip. Maurie helped them collect their belong-ings, and Mrs. Morehead gave her an impulsive hug as they said goodbye. "Don't let that nice Mr. O'Shane get away," she told her in a conspirator's whisper.

Mr. Morehead studied Maurie for a long moment as they shook hands. "You don't look well, girl. I don't think Ireland agrees with you," he said bluntly.

For some reason, Maurie felt a deep sense of loss as the couple drove away, which was ridiculous, she thought, because she'd hardly had anything but a passing acquaintance with them. Their superficial chatter had usually bored her, but there was something solid and unchanging about them that she would miss.

When Mrs. Duffy said she would be going to market midmorning, Maurie asked impulsively, "Would you mind if I went with you?" She didn't want to be alone. Tired and apprehensive, she needed the older woman's brisk, common-sense company.

Mrs. Duffy gave a light laugh. "Sure and I'd be glad to have someone come along. 'Tis a ten-mile drive, but Havenmoor has a farmer's market that makes it worth the trip. Can't depend only on lodgers to keep this old place going."

"I don't see how you manage all by yourself."

"Ain't easy. We used to have three men for day help when Mr. Duffy was alive. Now I'm down to one. Hard enough keeping a small truck farm going." She shook her head. "But there's plenty who envy me.

Lucky I am to have a roof over my head in these hard times.''

A middle-aged man, Mr. Cranby, who wore a black cap and baggy trousers, was her day help, and he loaded a battered old pickup with eggs, a half-dozen plucked chickens, a newly butchered pig and some early garden produce.

Mrs. Duffy gave the man instructions for the day and then climbed into the driver's seat of the old truck. Maurie had to slam her door twice to get it to shut.

Mrs. Duffy ground the starter to a point that Maurie despaired of it ever turning over, but finally the old truck rattled to life. Maurie held on to the seat as the truck bounced over the rutted road. Unconcerned, Mrs. Duffy maintained a loud, shouting conversation over the sputtering, backfiring engine.

"Was born a couple of miles over that next hill," she said with pride. "Married my childhood sweetheart and raised two strapping boys who have settled down on their own farms in County Cork. My husband, bless his soul, never was away for more than a day our whole married life. 'Tain't easy being alone.''

"Have you thought about marrying again?'' Maurie asked. A man her age would be lucky to have such a hardworking mate.

Mrs. Duffy sent her a disgusted look. "Never wanted anybody's shoes under my bed but my dear Joshua's, and I never will!''

That settled that.

Maurie lost all track of direction after a few miles down the country road. Rolling hills, rock-laced farms and empty spaces stretched to a horizon that strained the eyes. Yesterday's rain had left a sparkle of green upon the harsh, unforgiving land. No wonder they called it the Emerald Isle, she thought. A quiver of something like pride surprised her. It was foolish for her to feel a sense of home about a country she'd only known for a week.

On the outskirts of a village, they passed some kind of religious procession. A man in a clerical tunic carried a statue, and several nuns in wimples and robes herded a group of schoolchildren into an old church. The scene reminded Maurie of Tansie. What could have happened to cause the church to accuse a young woman of witchcraft?

Maurie turned to Mrs. Duffy. "What did Tansie do to be accused of being a witch?"

"They say she put a curse on someone and it came true."

"Who?"

"A man who was beating his young son. Tansie jerked the leather belt from his hand and said, 'May your arm be severed from your body for this evil.' The next day he lost his right arm in a peat cutter."

"Surely they couldn't condemn her for one incident!"

"Och, there were more. Some said she didn't know the power of the devil she had in her."

"Do you think she's . . . possessed?"

Mrs. Duffy shrugged. "Don't rightly know."

"Could she cast a spell on someone . . . to have terrible nightmares?"

"I suppose she could." The landlady sent her a long look. Then she drove for several minutes before adding, "But I don't rightly know why she would, do you?"

Maurie remained silent. Agreed, Tansie was strange, but she seemed purposeful. Her conversation was sharp and to the point. And there was a stubbornness about it. If the impossible were true—that she was causing the haunting nightmares—Maurie despaired of ever escaping the witchlike spell.

When they neared the hamlet where the market was held, the narrow road became congested with wagons, cars, trucks and bicycles. Some vehicles arrived empty to carry supplies back home; others were loaded like Mrs. Duffy's truck with produce to sell.

The landlady found a place to park in a field adjoining the open market, and Maurie helped her carry her wares to one of the long tables. There were greetings all round for Mrs. Duffy, and Maurie suspected that the day market was as much a social happening as anything else. No one seemed to mind the soggy chill left from yesterday's rain. It seemed enough of a blessing that the overcast day promised a few hours of clear weather.

"Just enjoy yourself, dear," said Mrs. Duffy with a dismissing wave of her hand.

Maurie wandered about watching customers barter over goods with good-natured stubbornness. Some buyers quickly made their purchases, loaded up their trucks and wagons and left. Early birds got the pick of the merchandise; some of the tables quickly emptied. She doubted there would be much left by noon. Then what? There would be the rest of the day to get through when they got back to the farm. Would Daylan be back?

Maurie pulled her thoughts away from a cauldron that was beginning to boil with doubts and suspicions. She was too tired to sort anything out now.

The smell of fresh bread drew her to a table loaded down with fresh pastries, and she bought a hot sugared bun. Holding it in a paper napkin, she wandered away from the center of the market. An ubiquitous rock fence lined the edge of the field. She sat down, leaning against the piled stones as she ate her pastry.

The sun had come out, chasing ragged ends of clouds away and bathing the landscape in a golden glow. A pair of skylarks sailed smoothly from tree to tree, darting like drops of liquid color against the deep green leaves. A mesmerizing peace settled on Maurie as she watched them.

She brought herself up with a jerk. No, she couldn't allow herself to go to sleep. Even as a sensible inner voice mocked her cowardice, she knew she had to keep fighting sleep the same way she had all night. Terror waited for her if she let herself slip back into that terrifying nightmare. She had to stay awake.

"Mrs. Fitzgerald. What are you doing here?"

Fitzgerald. The name was like a knife to her chest. She couldn't breathe. *I'm in the dream again.* She had lost the battle to stay awake.

Maurie stared at a young man who had stopped his bicycle a few feet from where she sat. He was a good-looking youth, dressed in jeans and a sweatshirt. A legion of freckles marched across his nose, and a baseball cap was set jauntily on the back of his wild, curly red hair. His basket was filled with bundles.

"You gave me quite a start," he said with a merry laugh. "Is Miss Doughty with you?"

The nurse! Fright swept up into Maurie's eyes. Was Miss Doughty nearby? With the doctor? She wanted to get to her feet and flee. Hysterical laughter bubbled up in her throat.

You can't outrun a dream.

"Mrs. Fitzgerald, are you all right?"

Maurie choked back the diabolical mirth. Remaining in control was very important. She moistened her dry lips. "Yes. Yes, I'm fine. Just tired."

At the sound of her voice, Maurie stiffened. She was speaking in her own American accent. Not the clipped

British speech that Dawna spoke in her nightmare. Maybe she wasn't asleep. Maurie's eyes fled past the youth to the bustling farmer's market. The scene had always shifted in her dream, but this setting was the same as when she was awake. Relief sped through her.

"I'm not Dawna Fitzgerald," she said eagerly to the young man. "And I'm not dreaming. I'm Maurie Miller, an American." This time her laugh was full and free. "Maureen Miller."

He edged away and said quickly, "Sorry, ma'am. My mistake."

"Don't you see? I'm wide-awake. I'm me."

He shoved down the pedal of his bike and sent the vehicle rolling quickly away from her.

"No!" she shouted, standing up. "Come back, come back!"

Giving a quick look over his shoulder, he pumped as fast as he could.

Maurie ran after him. "Stop! Please, stop!"

He was real, not a dream. He had called her Mrs. Fitzgerald. She had to talk with him. How could he know the woman in her dream?

"Please...please!" she gasped. "I have to talk with you."

She put everything she had into catching him. She bent her head and covered the ground in long strides. Her chest burned with pain. Her legs began to cramp.

"No, wait!" she called again.

He only pedaled faster. Long after he had disappeared behind a high hawthorn hedge, she kept running. When she came to a junction of several rutted paths, she stopped and looked helplessly in every direction.

No sigh of the youth. He was gone.

She fled down one lane, then came back and stumbled in another direction. Which way had he gone? She ran this way and that. The sensation was one of being lost in a nightmare with never-ending roads stretching away.

With an anguished cry, she finally collapsed to the ground. Covering her face with her hands, she sobbed. *Dear God. Am I awake or dreaming?*

CHAPTER ELEVEN

Maurie lifted her head when she heard the old truck rumbling down the narrow road toward her. For a moment she was completely disoriented. Her vision was fuzzy. Where was she? Why was she sitting on the ground? Sweat-dampened locks of hair hung down on her forehead, and her lips were dry and dusty. She'd been running. Now she remembered—the redheaded boy. He had called her Mrs. Fitzgerald. She'd wanted to talk with him, but he wouldn't stop. Had she fallen asleep? Was it only a minute ago that she had chased the young man on his bicycle to this fork in the road?

Am I dreaming?

Mrs. Duffy brought the pickup to a stop, flung open the door and hurried over to the side of the road where Maurie sat blurry eyed and heavy lidded.

The landlady's round face was furrowed and anxious. "Blessed Mother, 'tis a fright you were giving me. What ails you, girl? Rushing off like that, yelling and waving your arms like the dark furies were on your coattail." She touched her hand to Maurie's forehead. "Och, you're sweating like a pig on a spit."

Maurie moistened her lips. Had the horror passed? Was she herself again? *Please, please let me be Maureen Miller.*

"There now. Don't you worry none." Mrs. Duffy put a chubby arm around her and helped her to her feet. "That's it. Come on, girl. Get in the truck."

Maurie ran a clammy hand across her brow, trying to gather her wits. Everything that had happened was crystal clear—sitting by the wall, eating her pastry, and then the young man stopping his bike in front of her. That's when the nightmare must have began, she told herself as Mrs. Duffy turned the truck around.

"Thank you... for coming," Maurie managed apologetically.

"It's to a doctor we're going. No argument," Mrs. Duffy said flatly as Maurie tried to protest. "There's a good one in Havenmoor. I left someone watching my table. Caught up to you as fast as I could."

"Have I been gone long?" Maurie asked, her forehead furrowed in puzzlement.

"Just as long as it took to turn my table over to someone and come barreling after you. Not more than five minutes."

"I'm sorry," said Maurie, leaning her head back in the seat as Mrs. Duffy turned the truck around. "I... I don't know what came over me."

But she did. She remembered very clearly the young man addressing her as Mrs. Fitzgerald. *What are you doing here? Is Miss Doughty with you?* Maurie put a hand over her eyes.

Mrs. Duffy eyed her suspiciously. "I saw you sitting a ways off, eating and looking mighty contented. The next time I looked you were screaming and running down the road."

"Didn't you see the young man on the bicycle? He stopped right in front of me."

"I didn't see you talking with anyone, but I wasn't watching you every minute. Old man Dungan was trying to drive my price down on a chicken. Worst skinflint in the county, he is. I shoved my face into his and told him no respecting chicken would be caught stewing in his cheating pot." She gave a nod of satisfaction. "No, I didn't see you talking to no lad."

"He had curly red hair. His bike was blue."

"Doesn't ring a bell. But there were lots of people milling around."

I must have fallen asleep, thought Maurie. Resting against the stone wall, weary from a sleepless night, she had failed to stay awake and the nightmare had come back. Yes, she must have been drawn into the dream again, this time with a young man treating her as if she were Dawna Fitzgerald.

She pressed her fingers against her temples. Something was wrong with that rationalization. What was it? A nagging contradiction like a sharp-edged gear went round and round in her mind. An elusive truth was just beyond her reach.

Then she had it. She had always awakened from the nightmare in the same place where she had fallen asleep. But not this time. If she had been chasing the youth in her dream, why had she awakened at the side of the road, instead of against the rock wall where she had been resting? Running down the road in a dream would not have put her at a different place when she awakened. Unless she'd been sleepwalking. But if she'd been awake, then the encounter with the youth had really happened. But that was impossible. Dawna Fitzgerald belonged in her nightmare. She put her hand over her face and groaned.

Mrs. Duffy sent her an anxious glance. "It'll be all right. The doc'll fix you up in no time."

"Please, no need to go to all that trouble. I just have a headache, that's all. I'll take a couple of aspirin and be fine."

Mrs. Duffy didn't answer. She just pursed her lips and kept driving.

The woman was obviously ill at ease, thought Maurie. And no wonder. She's probably thinking her American boarder is on drugs, or worse, maybe even some kind of psychopath. Maurie's mind worked feverishly to invent some reasonable explanation for her wild behavior.

"I appreciate your concern, but I really don't need to see a doctor. I saw a young man steal a bike, and I ran after him trying to catch him. Unfortunately I ran out of steam—and he got away."

The way her landlady set her jaw, Maurie knew she recognized the lie for what it was. "'Twon't do any harm to have the doc check you out," she said flatly. "Sure 'tis you look ready to topple over if a morning wind shoved at your back."

Maurie discovered she was unable to make a forceful argument. A bone-deep weariness had sapped her strength. Her thoughts seemed to be lost in a fog.

"Tell him you're having trouble sleeping and eating and he'll fix you up with a sleeping potion. He gave me one when Joshua died. I found out you can't get through the days if you can't get through the nights."

Maybe Mrs. Duffy was right, thought Maurie. If the doctor prescribed a strong sedative, she might be able to sleep and get rid of her exhaustion. She'd always been critical of people who relied on medication for every little thing—but this was no little thing!

What if he tells me I'm losing my mind? What would happen to her? She decided right then that she wouldn't be honest with him. It would be safe enough just to admit she wasn't sleeping well. Nothing unusual about that he'd probably say—a strange country, a touch of homesickness. He'd give her some tranquillizers and she'd be herself again. The crazy dreams would go away as quickly as they had come. Yes, that's the way it would be. How could she believe anything else?

The village of Havenmoor lay at the foot of bare hills with nothing to soften the ridges but scraggly grasses. Weathered buildings clustered closely together as if seeking protection from the vast open spaces in every direction.

"My family home was about a mile down that road," Mrs. Duffy said as she drove down a narrow street where small businesses, barns and dwellings hugged a broken sidewalk.

Maurie wanted to say that Glenmara was more picturesque than Havenmoor, but she was afraid her landlady wouldn't appreciate the comparison. No one liked to have his hometown belittled.

She parked in front of a tobacconist's and led Maurie around the side of the building. Nothing on the outside door indicated a doctor's office, but Mrs. Duffy headed up the steep stairs as if she'd been there many times. Maurie wondered about the practicality of having a doctor's office that was so inaccessible to the injured.

A strong medical smell hovered in the air as they reached the second floor, and Mrs. Duffy led the way into a small front office already crowded with patients.

"The doctor is delivering a baby at the O'Keffee farm," a squarely built nurse-receptionist told them. "Don't know when he'll be in. You can wait if you like." She nodded toward a bench already amply filled with a mother and her two squirming youngsters.

Maurie was relieved the doctor was out. The prospect of answering a physician's questions had created much uneasiness. She would have left the office without a moment's hesitation if Mrs. Duffy hadn't put a firm hand on her arm. "Better that you wait."

"No, I—"

"I'll not be taking you home." There was a no-nonsense set to her chin.

Maurie knew it wouldn't do any good to argue. And maybe Mrs. Duffy was right. Maurie did need something to calm her nerves. "All right." She looked at her watch. She couldn't believe it was only nine o'clock in the morning. "Surely the doctor will be back before lunch."

"I'll go back to the market and see to my table. If you're through before I get things closed up, I'll pick you up at Callahan's down the street." With that, she turned and marched out the door, leaving Maurie standing in the middle of the room with a dozen curious eyes fastened on her.

"Find a seat," ordered the brisk nurse. Once again she nodded toward the crowded bench. The young mother moved over, holding the youngest child on her lap to make room for Maurie.

"Thank you," Maurie murmured as she sat down.

As time passed, she was only vaguely aware of the rustle of impatient feet, muffled coughing and the mother's tired admonitions to her restless children.

She mentally rehearsed what she would say to the doctor. *Please give me something to let me sleep without dreaming. I have this horrible...* No, she wouldn't mention her dreams. She'd have to be very careful. *I have trouble falling asleep and when I do...* Her stomach tightened with apprehension. What if he thought her mentally disturbed? No talk of tansy flowers and the strange woman's babble about a web of dreams. No mention of a dark brooding Oliver who made threats and filled her mind with doubts about the man she desired. She'd have to—

"The doctor's here," announced the nurse finally. There was a relieved rustle in the waiting room. She nodded to the young mother. "Mrs. Kiley, you're first."

The nurse held open an inner door. As the mother and her children filed through, Maurie glimpsed a long hall with doors leading off it. At the far end, she saw the doctor come out of his office. He was a tall, lean man, gray-haired and wearing dark-rimmed glasses on his slender nose. His mouth was held in a severe line, and even though she was too far away to see his eyes, Maurie knew they were the color of iced pewter. She had seen him before.

Dr. Thomas A. Ferges. Dawna's doctor.

The nurse closed the door and Maurie clutched the edge of the bench to keep from plunging forward in a dead faint. The last taut thread holding her to the reality of the moment snapped. She felt disembodied, floating. The walls of the waiting room wavered under her gaze as if they were underwater. The faces of the people staring at her were like reflections in a circus mirror, distorted and inhuman. *So I am mad,* she accepted with a strange kind of relief.

Slowly she rose to her feet, walked out of the room and down the narrow steps to the street. Shock had numbed her whole body. She just stood there on the sidewalk, purposeless, her brain chilled beyond coherent thought.

Several people brushed by her, but she wasn't even aware of their curious glances. The little street was busy with cars weaving their way around wagons, hand-drawn carts, and jaywalking pedestrians. A tour bus pulled to a stop almost directly in front of Maurie and began unloading. She just stood there as tourists flowed out, engulfing her in their chattering midst. An elderly woman was the last one out. "I just hate these long morning tours," she complained to Maurie. "Don't you? I'm ready for lunch. Come on or we'll be left with the dregs." She strode forward and Maurie followed.

No one else looked at her as the tourists swept into the old drinking house and scattered to sit at tables crowded together. The management must have been ready for the scheduled tour because waitresses immediately started scurrying about taking lunch orders and serving drinks.

Maurie took a seat at the end of a long table and ordered the same sandwich as the elderly woman sitting beside her, but when the waitress put it in front of her, the sight of the rare beef and sauerkraut turned her stomach. Instead of eating, she drank a mug of Guinness. Laughter, music and lively conversation flowed around her. A comely redhead strumming a guitar began singing an Irish folk song.

I slept last night in a barn at Curraghbawn,
A wet night came on and I skipped through the door,
Holes in me shoes and me toes peeping through,
Singin' skiddy-me-red-doodlum . . .
Must be getting home for i's gettin' late at night,
The fire's all raked and there isn't any light,
Singin' skiddy-me-red-doodlum . . .''

Maurie barely heard the rest of the lyrics, but she clapped when the others did. A numbing cocoon continued to protect her from a terror too great to be faced. When the lunch hour was over, the tourists scurried back to the bus. Maurie stood on the sidewalk and watched the vehicle drive away.

Like a mindless windup toy, she turned and started walking down the sidewalk. She had reached the corner when Mrs. Duffy's old pickup gave a snorting backfire as it pulled to the curb beside her. The landlady reached over and opened the door.

"There you be. I was on my way to Callahan's to collect you. The doctor must have seen you in good time. What'd he have to say?"

Maurie climbed into the truck. A sick chill made her lips tremble. The protective shock was easing away, leaving her vulnerable. Twice in one day she had lost touch with reality. There was no escape from her madness. No way to deny that her mind had betrayed her.

"Well, tell me, girl. What'd he say was wrong with you?" Mrs. Duffy looked at her suspiciously. "You did see the doctor, didn't you?"

She moistened her dry lips. "Yes, I saw him."

"And he gave you something for what ails you?"

Maurie turned haunted eyes on Mrs. Duffy. "I never did hear the doctor's name."

"Ferges," she answered with a puzzled look. "Thomas A. Ferges."

"But how could he be real?" Maurie said in a neutral tone that hid the dark despair washing over her. "How could I have known that he existed?"

"Because I told you about him." Her landlady sent Maurie an uneasy glance.

"When?"

"Today, when I took you to his office."

The spurt of hope quickly died. Maurie shook her head. "I knew him . . . before that. I knew what he looked like. I knew his name."

He injected a needle into my arm.

"What's the matter with you, girl? I'd think you were half-drunk if I didn't know better." She eyed Maurie. "You haven't been tossing down a few mugs, have you?"

"Just one Guinness." The drink set uneasily in her empty stomach. She should have eaten the sandwich.

"That's enough for anyone not used to strong ale," the older woman answered with satisfaction, as if she'd found sufficient reason for Maurie's peculiar behavior. "You'd better watch yourself. Turning to drink won't solve anything. Just creates a heap more problems."

Maurie kept her silence. Better let her think she had a secret drinker on her hands than a woman who hallucinates and can't tell a dream from reality.

"When we get back to the house, you'd better hightail it to bed and sleep it off," Mrs. Duffy said bluntly.

Sleep. The word brought a bead of sweat to Maurie's upper lip. She forced herself to look out the window, but the rolling countryside with its lowing sheep and grazing cattle was a mockery to the hurricane swirling inside her.

When they drove into the clearing behind the farmhouse, Maurie was slow in getting out of the truck. The shell-shocked feeling remained. She knew that she had to do something—but what?

The back door of the house opened, and Daylan hurried across the yard to her. One clear feeling arose out of the quagmire of her emotions as the soft gaze of his dark eyes met hers. Joy. The curve of his smile stilled her panic.

"There you are," he said. "I was wondering where you were."

She went into his arms. He held her quietly as she pressed her cheek against his chest. Then she raised her eyes to his.

"I have to get away from here," she whispered hoarsely. "I think I'm losing my mind."

CHAPTER TWELVE

Daylan drove at a leisurely speed as they headed south down the coast road. He spoke very little, but Maurie drew reassurance from the warmth of his body and the promising smile that hovered at the corners of his mouth. He had not questioned her frantic insistence that she had to get away from Glenmara; her wan face, trembling lips and haunted eyes had been enough to convince him of her distraught state.

"Sure and the girl has had a bit of an upset," Mrs. Duffy had told Daylan. "I did my best—taking her to Dr. Ferges and all. Pshaw, I don't know what's ailing her. Maybe a couple of days of sight-seeing will do her good."

Sight-seeing had not been what Maurie had on her mind as she hastily packed an overnight bag and joined Daylan in his car. Her frayed nerves were ready to snap. She knew that getting away offered a means of survival. She sat stiffly on her side of the seat, not looking at him or the scenery. She clasped her hands tightly in her lap and struggled to keep her mind blank.

They had been on the road about an hour when her taut muscles began to relax. Her tight breathing eased. She turned her head to look out at the Irish landscape touched with the luminous glow of the afternoon sun.

As if Daylan had been waiting for some sign that she was feeling calmer, he gave her a teasing smile. "Aren't you lonesome sitting way over there all by yourself?"

She smiled back, reassured by the tender persuasion in his question. Not demanding. Not forceful. Just warm and inviting. She moved closer to him, and he put an arm around her shoulder, driving one-handed down the two-lane highway.

They stopped for gas in a picturesque little village of quaint shops and pubs. The people meandering along the streets had an unhurried tranquil air about them. Somewhere a church bell tolled two o'clock.

Daylan glanced at his watch and then gave her a questioning look. "Have you had lunch?"

Her face clouded. The ragged edge of shock was still there. It all came back. The way she had clung to the tourists as if they could protect her from shattering into a thousand jagged pieces. She wanted to tell Daylan about the tour bus and the sandwich she'd ordered and couldn't eat, but the words wouldn't come.

He took one look at her ashen face and said, "Yes, we'll get something to eat here."

After parking the car, he took her arm and they walked across the street to a small café. A spattered menu presented limited choices. The cook's specialty was touted as delicious leek-and-potato soup with freshly baked scones.

Daylan ordered for both of them. "We'll start with the soup."

As Maurie slowly spooned the soup into her mouth, its warmth seeped into her tired, chilled body. She felt herself becoming whole again as the nourishment fueled her energy. She bit into the soft buttered bread with an intensity akin to a starving stray.

Daylan watched her with concern in his eyes. He made sure that her cup was kept filled with coffee, bitter, strong and invigorating. "Better?" he asked, with a gentle smile.

She nodded, holding the earthenware mug tightly with both hands as she sipped the steaming liquid. Slowly the color came back to her face.

"What are you trying to do to yourself by not eating? And from the look of those heavy eyes, not sleeping, either."

She kept her gaze lowered.

"What is it, Maurie? What did the doctor say is the matter?"

She moistened her lips. "I . . . I didn't see him."

"But Mrs. Duffy said—"

"I know. She took me to the doctor's office but . . . but I left before he saw me."

She took a slow sip of coffee before she answered. "Because he was the same horrid doctor I've been dreaming about."

"What?"

She locked eyes with Daylan and took a deep breath. "It's just like the nurse. She was in my dream, and then I saw her at the pub. Now, it's Dr. Ferges." Her voice quivered. "When I saw him today in his office, I ran."

Daylan covered her trembling hand with his. "Darling, we've been through this before. You must have seen the man at some time—"

"I haven't!" She clutched his hand, sinking her nails into his flesh. "I even knew his name. Thomas A. Ferges, M.D. In my dream it was printed in gold letters on his doctor's bag."

"There you go," he said with infuriating calmness. "Somewhere, sometime, you saw this doctor and his bag, and your subconscious replayed it in a dream. For some reason or another, love, you seem to have a fixation on doctors and nurses. Maybe it's because you're not feeling well and you're afraid you're going to get sick, alone in a strange country." He lifted her hand and brushed it lightly with his lips. "Only you're not alone."

She blinked back a sudden fullness in her eyes. "I don't know what's happening to me. Sometimes I don't know if I'm awake or dreaming."

"Dear one, you can be sure of one thing," he said, touching her cheek. "When you're with me, you're awake."

She wanted to tell him about the red-haired youth, but another weird confession might push him away. She was already stretching their relationship by behaving in such an irrational way.

"And you're going to forget about nightmares, nurses, doctors and everything else," he ordered. "I only want you to think about one thing."

"What's that?"

He drew her up from her chair and put his arm around her waist as they walked to the door. He whispered in her ear, "I'll show you—in due course."

She didn't know how far they were going or where they would stay the night. The rhythm of the car, the muffled whine of tires on the pavement and the beautiful landscape rolling by combined to ease her nerves. She dozed with her head on his shoulder.

A lavender twilight had fallen when he stopped at a small manor house. The bed-and-breakfast was set so close to a bay that the sound of lapping water could be heard in their small upstairs room. As soon as Daylan had deposited the bags in their room, he held her close for a moment. "You look too weary to go out for dinner. Why don't you enjoy a nice hot bath while I see about rustling up some food?"

She smiled at him gratefully. She wasn't up to being with people or engaging in polite conversation. All she wanted was to shut out the world and be alone with this man who could dominate her senses with a single look.

He kissed the tip of her nose. "I'll be back in two winks of a leprechaun's eye, my fair colleen," he said, in a deep dramatic voice. "We'll feast on ambrosia and nectar, and I promise that the fruits of love will bring a glow to yer cheeks and a sparkle to yer eye."

His youthful exuberance made Maurie laugh, and suddenly she was filled with giddy lightness.

"Hurry," she ordered.

While he was gone, she bathed in deliciously hot water, washed her hair with a complimentary lemon-scented shampoo and dried off with a soft towel. Standing naked beside her open suitcase, she looked with dismay at what she'd packed. Jeans and tops, underclothes and a high-necked grannie gown that she'd worn all last winter. Nothing appropriate to wear for a romantic feast of "ambrosia and nectar."

She was about to give in to jeans and a T-shirt when she spied Daylan's suitcase lying open on the bed. On top lay a soft, long-sleeved shirt of deep aquamarine.

She smiled and, with a mischievous glint in her eyes, took the shirt out of his suitcase and slipped it on. She loved the way the silk cloth whispered as it clung to her. The minute she had finished buttoning the shirt, she began to have doubts.

Her fingers hesitated on the collar as she saw her reflection in the mirror. Maybe he wouldn't want her wearing his things. Some men were very possessive, even about ordinary things like combs and brushes, let alone their clothes. She didn't know any little personal things about him. No insights about his moods in the morning or bedtime rituals. Although his outfits were casual and well fitted, she didn't know if clothes were important to him. Should she take the shirt off or not?

The decision was taken from her. A key turned in the lock, the door opened, and in he came, his arms loaded with paper sacks. He kicked the door shut with one foot, turned around and then froze.

"Oh, you're back," she said with a breathless nervousness.

His expression was unreadable as his gaze traveled from her breasts and down the long legs that showed below the short shirttail barely covering her fanny.

"I . . . I borrowed your shirt," she said needlessly.

"So I see," he said in a gruff voice. He placed the sacks on a nearby table. "And ye've a penalty to pay for it."

"What kind of . . . penalty?"

His smile was slow and devastating. "I'll show you." He drew her to him with the sure touch of a lover. His fingertips traced the curve of her cheek, and desire flamed in his eyes as he lowered his mouth to hers. The slow deep kiss ignited a flash of sensation within her. A heady flow of heat like a thousand tiny flames licked at her. Her senses were dominated by the feel of his chest against her breasts and the caressing touch of his hands. He worked her mouth, teasing her lips with his questing tongue. He lifted the edge of the shirttail. His hands molded the curve of her thighs, slipping downward until she thought she would die from intense longing.

"My lovely *leannan*." He breathed the Gaelic endearment for sweetheart as he drew her to the bed. His deft fingers quickly unbuttoned the shirt, slipping it sensually off her shoulders as he buried his lips in the soft crevice of her breasts. He tossed the shirt on the floor, and in the next minute his own clothes followed.

Even though she had lain with him before, her surrender seemed brand-new. She held him to her with a fierceness that locked her to the powerful length of his body. As his flesh became hers, all her shattered emotions were mended. All her fears were banished. She felt whole. The zenith of fulfillment and the endearments he breathed as he made love to her were like a mystical power that made her a greater whole than herself. And when he slipped from her, she lay in the circle of his arms like someone freed from mortal bonds. With a deep sigh, she closed her eyes and curled herself against him.

She didn't know how long she'd been asleep when she awoke lazily to shadows dancing on the ceiling.

She languidly stretched out, content, until she realized that she was alone in the bed. She lurched to a sitting position. A fire blazed in a small fireplace, sending a radius of burnished light upon a man who sat with his back to her. Dark hair curled around the collar of a blue robe as he spread a cloth on the floor between them and the fireplace.

Where was she?

She bit her lower lip as the familiar thrust of panic surged through her. Before she could order her thoughts, he slowly turned his face toward her.

Oliver or Daylan?

Uncertain light played on his face, touching his dark eyes and the blue black of his hair. There was no dark mustache on his upper lip as he smiled at her. "I was just about to wake you, my beautiful *leannan*. Your midnight feast awaits."

Daylan! Tears of relief filled her eyes. She wasn't dreaming. The moment was real. Her lover was reaching for her, drawing her warm, nude body from the bed.

He kissed her possessively as she slipped her arms around his neck and threaded her fingers through his thick hair. He groaned and reluctantly loosened her arms. Then he picked up the discarded shirt and handed it to her. "You'd better put this on or I'll not be responsible for starving you to death. Come sit down."

He led her to the fireplace where a checkered table-cloth was spread on the floor and a single rose stood in a bud vase. He had bought wine, cheese, fresh fruit and a loaf of homemade bread.

"Wonderful," she breathed, easing down on the floor and folding her legs up under her in Indian fashion. Never again would such common food taste like pure culinary delight, she thought as she ate greedily, allowing him to keep her glass filled with a smooth white wine.

His deep brown eyes shone like imported cognac. Rich, mesmerizing and dangerous. As he lounged on the floor across from her, the blue robe scarcely covering his torso fell open in a tantalizing way that forced her to keep her gaze elevated. All the passion and desire that had lain dormant for the twenty-nine years of her life had exploded into feelings she didn't know she had. She was beyond acknowledging that she was playing Russian roulette by being utterly besotten by this man. Something had happened to sensible, always-in-control Maureen Miller.

"I bet you were the kind of little girl who never dared to take off her shoes and run barefoot through the grass."

She was startled by his astute comment. "Why... why would you say that?"

"Because you're sitting there, enjoying every sip of wine, your eyes glowing with remembered passion, and yet a guarded, guilty tension comes through in your body language.''

She gave a self-mocking chuckle. ''I never could steal from the cookie jar without experiencing a guilty stomachache afterward.'' She met his eyes boldly. ''But with practice I think I could take my pleasures without a flicker of moral conscience.''

''I wonder,'' he said thoughtfully.

''I don't understand. Why do you think I'm not at ease with what's happened between us? I assure you I've been on a weekend date before. When I was in college, I was engaged to a young lawyer in my father's firm.''

''And?''

''And I decided not to marry him.''

''Why?''

''I'm not quite sure. It just didn't seem to matter whether he was in or out of my life. So I decided *out* was better.'' She held out her glass for more wine. ''What about you? Any near trips to the altar?''

Her lips trembled as she waited, searching his eyes for the truth. Would she know if he lied to her? What if he told her he was married? Confessed that he went home to a wife on those nights he was away from the boardinghouse?

''Don't be so apprehensive. You look like a young doe facing a gun, waiting to be shot.'' He moved the soft shirt above her breasts and loosened the belt on his robe. She accepted his wonderful taking with joyous relief. All the need for answers or denials fled as they made love again.

When he carried her sleepy body to bed, she slipped into a contented slumber that defied any nightmarish intrusions.

After a leisurely breakfast provided by the owner of the manor house, they spent the day enjoying a circular trip around the Dingle Peninsula, the most westerly point in Ireland. Maurie was startled to find that most of the inhabitants in the area spoke Gaelic. In small villages, they encountered several groups of students and civil servants trying to learn the language, and Daylan seemed right at home, exchanging greetings with them and laughing as they struggled for command of the foreign tongue.

"My grandfather was born and raised here," Daylan said, offering a rare insight into his family. "He married my grandmother and they lived in a cottage near the town of Dingle until they decided to move north." His face grew dark. "Better that they'd never left."

"What did your grandfather do?"

"He was a skilled maker of curraghs. Finest fishing boats afloat. A man in Ulster offered him a job, so he and my grandmother raised their family in Northern Ireland. My father went to Trinity College and married my mother, a childhood sweetheart. My sister and I were raised in Dublin and spent a lot of time with our grandparents. Grandpa loved to come back here to Dingle once a year and rove the beaches and climb the mountains. When he died, I wanted to bury him here, but there wasn't enough left of his body to fill a basket. He was blown to bits by the same explosion that took my sister's life.''

She touched his arm, but words wouldn't come. There was no way to ease the tortured emotions that played behind his shuttered eyes. In a moment, his expression eased and he was in control again. ''This area has a wealth of early Christian churches and Norman castles. Come, I'll show you a good example of a Hiberno-Romanesque church of the twelfth century.''

At Kilmalkedar, they walked through the ruins of the old church. A weather sundial still stood amid inscribed stones, and neither Daylan nor Maurie spoke as spirits dead some eight hundred years seemed to be carried on the hushed wind.

They stopped at Danequin for a wonderful lunch of fresh oysters and baked salmon. Daylan chatted easily with a seaman who was offering his boat for a trip out to the deserted Blasket Islands. That might be fun, thought Maurie, but Daylan didn't seem inclined to accept the man's offer. Maurie wished she could understand more of what was being said, but Daylan repeated bits and pieces for her. She was more than willing for him to take charge.

"How about a swim in Tralee Bay?" he asked her, as they reached a small resort town of Castlegregory in late afternoon.

"I didn't bring a bathing suit."

"Begorra, 'tis a sorry thing that no nude bathing is allowed," he said with teasing solemnity. "But I'll wager you could find a wisp of a suit at one of the shops that would do justice to those delectable curves of yours."

They checked in at one of the comfortable hotels. A small shop off the lobby offered a limited choice of bathing suits. Daylan gave his approval to a white bikini that under different circumstances she would have thought scandalous.

"Come on—let's see if that suit shrinks."

His own trunks were black and hugged low on his hips. As they ducked each other playfully in the water, she hooked her fingers on the elastic band and dropped his trunks before he could react.

Laughing, she tried to get away from him, but in the end, she surrendered as he pulled her behind the seclusion of some protective rocks and evened the score. That night they were like honeymooners, oblivious to the world beyond the one in each other's arms.

The next morning, as Daylan brushed back the hair that had drifted forward on her cheeks, he said, "I'm sorry, my *annsachd,* my darling. I could live in paradise with you forever. Unfortunately we have to go back." His voice was sad. "I have commitments."

She was too much of a realist to expect the idyll to go on forever. She had no right to make any more demands on him, now or in the future. He had already given her more than she could ever repay. "I understand," she quickly assured him, as the wonderful warm feeling began to recede. "I don't know what I would have done without you."

"You've changed your mind about going home right away, haven't you?"

She cupped his strong jaw and touched her fingertips to his lips. *How could I leave you now?*

He kissed each of her fingers. "Promise that you won't run off—no matter what happens."

"I promise." The commitment came easily in the throes of love.

They drove north and stopped for lunch in a busy pub very much like the one that had catered to the tourists in Havenmoor, only this one was filled with workingmen. Maurie felt a bit out of place in the smoke-filled, male-dominated bar. She was surprised that Daylan had chosen it. He gave their order rather briskly, and Maurie had the feeling he was impatient for their holiday to be over.

She tried several topics of conversation, but her relaxed, entertaining companion was gone. A dark, guarded solemnity had settled in his eyes. Was this the same man who had prepared a midnight picnic, complete with wine and a red rose? As Daylan sat across from her, eating in silence, he seemed like a stranger, and she felt a dark cloud settling over her.

Pushing back her plate, she excused herself to go to the ladies' room. As she washed her hands, a small mirror showed worry lines around her eyes. The rosy blush of love was already fading. The reprieve she'd been given was over. As she stared at herself, a hint of hardness crept into the set of her mouth. Time to take stock of herself. No more hysterical behavior. No more talk of spells and nightmares. She was herself again and ready to deal with any future confusing happenings in an unemotional manner. The halcyon hours she'd spent with Daylan had provided her with emotional armor.

Her soft smile turned into a frown as she returned to their table and found it empty. Daylan was probably freshening up, she thought. She was about to sit down and wait when she looked across the room and saw him heading out a side door of the tavern.

Where was he going? Why was he leaving without her? She was uncertain if she should stay or follow him. After a moment's hesitation, she began to weave her way around the crowded tables, heading for the side exit.

When she reached the outside door, she cautiously pushed it open. She stepped outside and surveyed a small courtyard that seemed to be more of a storage area than anything. A stone path lay close to the building, leading to the front of the pub in one direction and to a garage at the rear.

Daylan. She saw him at the side of the small building talking to two men—the same burly, rough-looking pair he'd met before. Now she knew why they had come to this particular pub for lunch. This meeting had been arranged—in secret.

She pulled back into the tavern, let the door shut and made her way back to their table with unanswered questions whirling in her head. These men had nothing to do with arranging for a consignment of lace, she would bet her life on it. He had been lying to her then, and he was deftly deceiving her again.

"Another drink, miss?" asked the harried waitress as she passed by with a tray of empty glasses.

Maurie shook her head. "My bill, please."

She pushed her way out of the tavern. She wanted to get out of the place, clear her head, have a chance to think and get her emotions under control. She crossed the narrow street and sat down on a small wooden bench that had been placed to give a view of the ocean.

Nettled questions tore at her. What is he up to? His behavior verified that it was something illegal. Mrs. Duffy had told her that secret societies like the Avengers were still operating. Some of their members were known to be terrorists, planting bombs, killing innocent people. All in the name of revenge. She also knew that Daylan had reason to be filled with hate because of his sister's and grandfather's deaths.

She stiffened when she heard footsteps behind her.

He touched her shoulder. "There you are. Sorry, I got waylaid. Are you ready to go?"

She moistened her dry lips. "Where were you?"

He eased her up from the bench and slipped her arm through his. "Oh, I had to make a couple of telephone calls. Business, you know."

CHAPTER THIRTEEN

Most of the return trip was spent in silence with sporadic exchanges of superficial comments about the landscape. Daylan offered a few historical tidbits, but he must have known she wasn't listening because after a while he gave up. A couple of times he tried to get her to sit closer to him so he could drive with one arm around her shoulder as he had for most of the trip, but she kept a cool distance between them. He raised a questioning eyebrow and said something facetious about lunch not agreeing with her.

"You're right about that," she answered with a steady look that challenged him to pursue the subject. He didn't. Only the cleft at the bridge of his nose deepened.

She bit her lip, turned away and stared unseeingly out the window. A desolate feeling settled in the pit of her stomach.

When they reached the farmhouse about dusk, he parked the car under the makeshift carport. Before she could open her door, he reached over and pulled her into his arms. Any protests rising to her lips were drowned in the swell of desire ignited by his kisses. The emptiness she'd felt a moment ago vanished like frost under radiant sunshine. She clung to him, forgetting his lies, responding to his devouring mouth and plunging tongue with a fierceness that brought a husky moan from his throat.

He raised his lips from hers. "We'd better be going inside."

"No," she said stupidly, as if that simple word could hold back reality forever.

He put a hand on each side of her face and held it tenderly. "I want you to remember something, my lovely Maureen, my dear *leannan*. After the rain . . . a rainbow."

Her face registered her puzzlement, but he only kissed the tip of her nose and was out of the car. She followed him as he carried their suitcases into the house through the kitchen.

Mrs. Duffy was obviously glad to see them back. "Well, look who's here. In time for my kidney pie." She quickly wiped her floured hands on her apron and gave Maurie a hug. "Did you have a good time, lass?"

Maurie nodded, hoping that the heat surging up in her cheeks didn't show.

"Sure and a couple of days' rest did you good," the landlady pronounced, eyeing Maurie's high color. "Not that I hold with young people behaving the way they do nowadays."

Daylan just laughed and kissed the older woman's pink cheek. "Don't be pretending you're not a renegade at heart. We went off with your blessing and you know it."

She waved him away with a twinkle in her eye. "Get on with you. And don't be wasting your silken blarney on the likes of me."

"What's been happening while we were gone?" he asked, helping himself to a couple of slices of dried apples set out for a pie.

"I rented the room the Moreheads had. Barely had time to turn it out before these two ladies were at the door." She gave a satisfied bob of her head. "Don't need to spend money advertising. Good word gets around. Someone at the airport recommended my place. Two lovely American ladies, they are. Both stewardesses."

Daylan raised an eyebrow. "Stewardesses?"

She nodded. "They had a few days' layover and wanted to get away from those places near the airport." She smiled at Maurie. "They'll be good company for you. Why don't you join them in the sitting room and get acquainted?"

"Good idea," agreed Daylan as he nodded at Maurie. "I'll take the bags up and then join you."

She would have preferred choosing her own time to meet the new boarders, and she resented the way Mrs. Duffy and Daylan seemed to be shoving her at them.

"All right," she said in neutral tone. It was just her mood, she chided herself, trying to shrug off her irritation. With a firm smile on her face, she went down the hall to the sitting room and introduced herself to the two new boarders.

"Mrs. Duffy told us about you," said the tallest of the women with an easy smile. "I'm Reva Jefferson and this is Bette Clampet."

"Maurie Miller." They shook hands all around and made light talk for a couple of minutes.

Both women were from Atlanta, Georgia, and were blond and very attractive. Bette carried a little extra weight that nicely curved her bust line and hips. Reva was trim, athletic and long legged. They were an outgoing pair, with the kind of get-acquainted friendliness cultivated by contact with lots of people for short duration.

As they chatted about their gypsylike life-style, Maurie had to do very little but smile and nod. When Daylan came down to join them, she didn't even have to do that. She could have left the room and neither woman would have noticed.

Daylan responded easily to their attentions. *He's used to having women fawn over him*, thought Maurie, withdrawing into a shell of silence during dinner. No one but Daylan seemed to notice. He tried to include her in the conversation, but like a pouting child, she answered in monosyllables. She didn't know whether it was Daylan or the bubbly young women who suggested a ride into town after dinner.

"We'd love to do a little pub-crawling," said Reva.

"Especially with such a handsome escort," added Bette with a flirtatious smile.

Daylan turned to Maurie. "What do you think, *leannan*? Are you up to a couple of nightcaps?"

Like the ones we had last night in our room at Castlegregory? The pain of remembering was too sharp and his use of the Gaelic endearment made the constraints between them even worse.

"No, I'm tired," she answered quickly. "I think I'll turn in."

As the two laughing women hugged his sides like bookends, Daylan held her gaze for a long moment and she was instantly contrite. Why had she been churlish? So uncommunicative? Only her pride kept her from asking him not to go.

"We'll bring him back safe and sound," promised Reva.

"Sweet dreams, Maurie," he said. *Would he come to her room later?* "See you in the morning, *mianna*."

"Yes, in the morning," she echoed. With your warm body wrapped around mine. Your dark head crowding my pillow. Soft unruly hair brushing my cheek, and the soft murmur of contented breathing in my ear.

She turned away quickly, a hungering ache tightening her chest. In her room, she mechanically emptied her bag and put everything back in the drawers and small closet.

The room was just as she had left it, only it had shrunk in size. It seemed much smaller and the air was stuffy and close. She missed the fresh sea breeze of the past two nights, the salty smell of brine and sand, the soft lullaby sound of lapping waters. She managed to raise the window a couple of inches. Then she sat on the floor and rested her head on the wide, old-fashioned windowsill. She knew she should go to bed. A suspicion that Daylan had welcomed an excuse to leave the house nagged her. She didn't want to think about his duplicity. Her feelings for him overrode everything else—even her good sense.

Just like your mother, an inner voice mocked.

Maurie's lips trembled. Was history repeating itself? Was Daylan O'Shane another Jake Flintery? Was she as blind as Maelene had been? Loving a man who took human life under the banner of just revenge?

After the rain . . . a rainbow.

What did he mean by that? What was he trying to tell her? Her mind wrestled with the poetic words and failed to understand their hidden meaning.

I'll stay awake until he comes home, she told herself, refusing to admit that at the back of her mind was an insidious fear. *If I go to sleep, I'll dream.* Even though she clung to the assurance that everything had changed now that she had found love, she was afraid to put the conviction to the test.

Daylan would know that her door was unlocked, and she was certain that after the gregarious Southern gals had settled in for the night, he would come to her. She would lie contented and safe in his arms. There would be no nightmare.

Night sounds reached her ears through the open window. A breeze rustled dark ivy vines clinging to the roof. Somewhere a bird whistled mournfully to a mellow moon.

Her head came up with a jerk and she knew she'd been asleep. The sound of muffled laughter in the hall outside her door must have awakened her. They were back. She could hear the closing of a bedroom door across the hall where the American women were staying.

Her body was stiff as she got to her feet. Through the open window she heard a car starting up, and a beam of headlights sliced across her window. Daylan's car! He had dropped off the boarders and was leaving again.

She pressed her face against the window and glimpsed fading lights as the car disappeared down the road—away from town.

All right, wise up, girl, she scolded herself. What choice do you have? Either accept the fact that you have to let him set the pattern of the relationship, or pack your bags and head back to your solitary life in Connecticut. She knew which one she should do.

She lay with her moist cheek against the pillow and finally fell asleep. Sometime during the night she lurched awake with a frightening cry. Her ears strained to hear loud, threatening footsteps coming closer. But an undisturbed silence told her she'd been dreaming again.

He wasn't at breakfast when she went down, so she knew that he hadn't come back all night.

"Oh, there you are!" bubbled Bette. "You should have come with us last night. You really missed a good time."

Reva nodded. "Daylan took us to several places." She lowered her voice. "I have to tell you I was a little uneasy at one of them. If he hadn't been with us, I'd have been shaking in my sneakers."

"A real dump, if you ask me," Bette added. "And the men and women were all talking in a language I couldn't understand."

"Gaelic, I think." Reva gave a nervous laugh. "Some of those weirdos looked as if they hadn't caught up with the twentieth century yet."

Like the men Daylan was meeting in secret? Maurie's stomach tightened with anxiety. What were they planning? Some horrible terrorist attack? With Daylan in the middle of it? He was a dangerous man with burning revenge in his heart. She'd known it from the beginning. There were two sides to his personality. She knew the gentle, caring and loving side, but she had glimpsed a fierce other behind his mask. Had the deaths of his sister and grandfather built a satanic vengefulness in him that would destroy others, as well as himself?

"We ended up at Kelly's Place," chuckled Bette. "What a crowd. Everybody within fifty miles seemed to be there. Have you been there?"

That's where I saw Miss Doughty. Maurie only half listened to Betty's chatter as her thoughts sped off in a different direction. Could Dr. Ferges have been there that night, too? Had she seen him and his black bag as she pushed through the crowd and later recalled it in her dream? Daylan was right. It must have happened that way. It was the only thing that made sense. Why else would she have dreamed about him before she saw him in his office?

Mrs. Duffy bustled into the dining room. "Oh, Maurie, if you've finished, Tansie's in the kitchen. Wants to have a word with you."

Maurie didn't move. Her first reaction was a desire to push back her chair and flee upstairs without a moment's hesitation. She wanted nothing to do with the woman.

"Didn't you want to ask Tansie some questions about Maelene O'Mallory?" Mrs. Duffy asked as Maurie made no sign of getting up.

Maurie considered. "Yes, I did," Tansie did have information about her mother, but maybe it would be better *not* to hear any more about Maelene O'Mallory. For heaven's sake, mocked an inner voice, what are you afraid of learning?

Maurie moistened her dry lips. She already knew the worst about her parentage. Once the information got battered about on the local grapevine, she'd certainly have to leave Glenmara. She wouldn't be surprised if Father Sashoney's housekeeper hadn't already spread the story about.

Maurie touched a napkin to her mouth, excused herself and took several deep breaths as she walked into the kitchen. Tansie was sitting in the same old chair by the stove, the spray of yellow flowers pinned to her gray sweater. Her eyes were like shiny black beads in her weathered face, and there was no hint of a smile on her thin lips as Maurie said hello.

"Ye ran off," she accused in a razor-sharp tone. "I prepared the way for ye and ye took to yer heels."

"I don't know what you're talking about," Maurie retorted briskly. "And I don't intend to waste my time trying to understand your double-talk."

Tansie's mouth flicked in what might have been an amused smile. "Ye've come to the well to drink, haven't ye?"

Her meaning was clear. If Maurie wasn't too much of a coward to reach for it, Tansie offered the knowledge she had come to Ireland to get.

"All right," Maurie said with a nod of concession. "I know you were a novice at the Catholic home and orphanage."

Tansie neither nodded nor blinked in response. She was like a night bird—waiting, watching, listening.

"You were with my mother when I was born," Maurie continued. "Tell me about her. Please." A lump caught in her throat. "Please, anything."

After a moment Tansie said in a crackling murmur, "She loved ye."

Maurie's eyes misted. "But I was only three days old when she died."

"Are ye believing that love is measured in hours?" Her question chided Maurie's ignorance.

"No, of course not." Maurie knew that enduring love just was—without beginning and without end. "And she loved my father?"

"Sure and her love was as strong as a gale in the sails of a curragh. And at the end her spirit flew to him with the ease of a white dove in flight."

"Thank you . . . for telling me."

Tansie's coal black gaze bore into Maurie's misty eyes. "'Tis a warning I gave ye. Ye cannot run away."

"I don't understand."

"Ye cannot run away from a part of yerself."

As Maurie stared into Tansie's mesmerizing dark eyes, the pungent odor of the tansy flowers touched her nose. A powdery dust, a whirl of yellow haze, seemed to swirl between herself and the hypnotic woman.

Maurie stumbled back, putting her hands on the kitchen table to keep from falling. Her knees threatened to buckle under her. She sat down weakly in one of the chairs and put her head in her hands.

When the dizziness passed and she looked up again, the chair by the stove was empty.

She sucked in deep breaths to still the wild battering in her chest. Her stomach churned with bitter nausea. She stumbled out of the kitchen.

Reva and Bette were still sitting at the dining room table, an array of tourist pamphlets spread out in front of them. They said something to her, but there was such a roaring in her ears that she fled past them into the hall without answering.

When Mrs. Duffy saw Maurie, she held out the hall phone. "Maurie. It's Mr. O'Shane. He wants to speak with you."

For a moment, Maurie just stared at the landlady as if she hadn't understood. Then she took the receiver in her sweaty hand. Her voice croaked a hello.

"Maurie, *leannan,* is that you? You sound funny."

She took a deep breath. "It's me."

"Is something wrong?"

Wrong? A hysterical wave of mirth threatened to answer his question. Maurie fought back an impulse to describe the confusion and bewilderment she'd just experienced in the kitchen. What if she told him that Tansie had warned her about running away from herself and had made her sick and woozy with those damn tansy flowers of hers? Maurie knew what his reaction would be. He'd only chide her for being foolish enough to pay any attention to the woman.

"No, nothing's wrong," she managed in an even tone. "Where did you spend the night?" She found satisfaction in mounting an attack. "I heard you bring the boarders home and then drive off again."

"Business."

"What kind of business keeps you out all night?"

"What is this? The third degree? Here I am calling to ask you out for a gala evening, and you sound ready to peel the skin from my bones." His voice softened. "If we're going to fight, *mianna,* let's do it tonight when we're close enough to enjoy making up. I hated spending the night away from you, love."

The velvet softness of his deep voice was like a caress. The remembrance of his touch brought a warm rippling to her skin, and breathlessly she said, "I missed you, too." Her longing to be with him again challenged her pride and found it wanting. She'd already forgiven him.

"I'll be back at the farm about six o'clock. Be ready for a celebration."

"Celebration? What are we celebrating?"

"Us. And I've found the perfect place. Cullen Castle. You'll love it. A sumptuous medieval feast. Music, song, wine and pageantry." His voice thickened. "Sure and the gods will be jealous if m'lady honors me with her company for this gala celebration."

She found herself laughing. "M'lady would be honored."

"Till tonight then." There was an intimate promise in his tone.

"Tonight." She remembered the picnic he had arranged in the room the first night of their romantic escape and the lovemaking that had followed. A quiver of anticipation made her voice husky as she said goodbye. She was filled with a warm glow as she put the phone down and leaned against the hall wall. Tonight. She would be with him again tonight. But there was a whole day to get through first.

Later in the morning, Reva knocked on her bedroom door. "Bette and I are going to walk into the village and do a little shopping. Want to come along?"

"Yes, I'd love to." The prospect of spending the day alone didn't hold any joy for her. Besides, she hadn't had a chance to look over Glenmara since her arrival, and it might be fun to take in some of the shops. The walk would keep her occupied—and awake.

From the pace Reva and Bette set, Maurie knew that both of them were daily joggers. She was a walker. They bragged about chalking up at least three miles a day. Maurie soon realized that her leisurely walks across campus hadn't put her in the shape to handle the pace these two set. She vowed that when she returned home she'd enroll in an exercise program.

Home. She turned the word over in her mind, trying to find some meaning in it. She pushed the nettled word aside. She wouldn't think about anything beyond today. *Beyond tonight.*

It didn't take long for the three of them to cover the picturesque business district. A few shops offered items for tourists, and Maurie replenished some of her toiletries.

Reva and Bette stopped at the Shamrock Touring Company, and Maurie wandered on down the street. The strong odor of tobacco floated out to the sidewalk, and she stopped in front of a small pipe-and-tobacco shop.

What had happened to Daylan's pipe? During the two days they'd spent together, he hadn't smoked it once. In fact, she couldn't *ever* remember seeing it lighted. She frowned. There had been a faint odor of smoke in some of his clothes. Was he, in fact, a cigarette smoker? *Like Oliver?*

As she stared into the tobacconist's window, the reflection of a limousine pulling to the curb behind her caused her to turn around. A chauffeur hopped out, came around the car and stood and waited by the passenger door.

Maurie looked about but didn't see anyone on the crowded sidewalk who looked prosperous enough to be waiting for a limousine. Just then a gray-haired woman holding a small child came around the corner, and the chauffeur quickly sprang to attention.

The little girl looked over the nanny's shoulder and directly into Maurie's eyes. Her little mouth wrinkled up and she gave a piercing cry.

Maurie couldn't move. Hollie. *I'm in the dream again.* She watched the nanny hush the child as they climbed into the car and the chauffeur closed the door behind them. He returned to the driver's seat. The long car drove off.

Wake up. Wake up. Maurie hugged herself. A soft whimpering came from her throat. People brushing by her sent her puzzled looks.

She waited for someone to stop and call her Dawna. *I won't be her. I won't.* She reached up and touched her hair, expecting to find it flowing long and free on her shoulders, but one side was tucked behind her ear and the other side lay in a soft flip against one cheek.

"Sorry we took so long, Maurie." Reva touched her arm. "Couldn't make up our minds about which tour to take."

"Ready for the walk back?" asked Bette. "Maurie, you look bushed. Maybe we should see if there's a taxi in this place."

Maurie stared at the two women. She wasn't dreaming. They called her Maurie. There wasn't any question about her being fully awake.

"I saw them. I saw them!" she said in a defiant tone. She took a few steps down the sidewalk, searching for a glimpse of the gray limousine, but it had disappeared from sight.

CHAPTER FOURTEEN

Maurie was ready when Daylan returned to the boardinghouse that evening to pick her up. She had decided not to tell him about seeing Hollie and her nanny getting into the limousine. She knew he would just insist that somewhere, sometime, she'd seen the little girl and motherly woman, and her subconscious had given them back in her nightmare. She knew it was the only logical explanation, but she no longer believed in logic. Everything that had happened since her arrival in Ireland had been anything but logical. Even her passion for Daylan was a wild craziness that defied every facet of her sensible nature.

When he walked into the sitting room, handsomely dressed in dark trousers, tweed jacket, white shirt and crimson tie, she forgot everything else but the joy of being in his company. He radiated the kind of sensuality and masculine virility that made her feel utterly feminine. Warmth swept up into her cheeks as he sent an approving glance over her red silk blouse, wide black suede belt and long multicolored quilted skirt. She had swept up her hair into a French roll and had chosen dangling earrings of gold and pearls.

He took her hand and let his gaze caress her as he looked down into her eyes. "I've missed ye, my *luasidh*, my lovely colleen."

She would have gone unabashedly into his arms if Reva and Bette hadn't come through the door at that moment, shattering the intimacy like a mallet upon crystal.

"Wow. Awesome!"

"Love that tie."

Maurie stood by with a forced smile on her lips as the two pretty stewardesses gushed over him. He laughed and responded with a light banter, teasing them in the same way he had the redheaded cigarette girl at Kelly's Place. His flirtatious charm was light, flattering and very effective—leaving the object of his attentions wanting more. He was practiced at handling the admiration of the opposite sex, thought Maurie, watching him accept compliments with a modest air that only validated his handsomeness.

Had he spent last night alone? Since he hadn't changed clothes at the farmhouse, he must have another place in the village, she realized, and a chill threatened to chase away the warmth his presence had brought. Possessive feelings about a man were new to her. *Steady, girl,* she cautioned. *Don't let jealous dragons run awry.*

"And you look lovely tonight, Maurie," Bette said, with an envious glance at Maurie's small waist and pleasing bust line.

"Much better than this afternoon," Reva added. "I was a little concerned about you."

Daylan frowned. "Did something happen this afternoon?"

Maurie shook her head and gave a light laugh. "Nothing except these two wore me out with their fast-paced jog into Glenmara. They made me realize how out of shape I am. From now on, it's a daily run for me."

Daylan studied her and she wondered if her forced, breezy answer had fooled him. She was glad when he offered her the short coat she'd left lying on her chair. His hands lingered on her shoulders long enough to express a promised intimacy. "Shall we go, m'lady? A medieval feast awaits."

"Yes, m'lord." She smiled and slipped her arm through his.

In the car, he drew her close and kissed her with a hunger that matched her own. She touched his cheek and felt the quickly beating pulse in his throat. If he'd wanted to ruin her coiffure with his fingers, she would have let him. But after kissing her until her lips were tingling, he drew away. His own breath was uneven and his smile regretful. "We'd best be off."

The drive up the coast would take about twenty minutes. Half listening to the radio's mellow music, she was content to sit quietly at Daylan's side, his teasing hand occasionally playing along her leg. The night sky was lovely, clear and spangled with stars. A night for lovers, she thought. All her desires were centered on the man who sat beside her. She was able to put aside all confusion, all apprehension and lose herself in the moment. She couldn't stifle a tinge of regret when a blaze of lights heralded their arrival at Cullen Castle.

"Well, here we are," Daylan said, turning off the main road and following a circular drive that was beautifully landscaped with trees, scrubs and a picturesque bridge over a stream bordered with low rock walls.

As the car emerged from a thick drift of trees, Cullen Castle rose up before them. Built of gray stone, the structure stood dramatically against the night sky, dominating the shoreline and sea. A rounded tower at each corner of the main building rose above a jagged, steep roof.

"Built as a fortress by the first earl of Cullenmore," Daylan told her. "It was attacked many times throughout the centuries. Even Oliver Cromwell had a go at it, but the castle never fell. Thousands of loyal subjects died defending it."

He stopped in front of the castle where a drawbridge led to a mammoth wooden door guarded by two knights in armor. Daylan helped Maurie out of the car and gave an attendant the keys for valet parking.

"Impressive, isn't it?" said Daylan, smiling at her expression as she stood in awe. "A descendant of the Cullenmore family refurbished the whole structure, put in central heating, modern windows and other luxuries. He created some private apartments that he leases at exorbitant rates. These elaborate medieval banquets bring in hordes of tourists. I hope you enjoy yourself.''

Something began to stir at the back of Maurie's mind. A nebulous sense of familiarity pricked at her. Private apartments? In a castle? Images of an elegant bedchamber and period furniture were crisp and clear in her mind's eye. Suddenly her chest felt tight. Cymbals clashed in her ears. She forced her eyes upward to the third floor where mullioned windows reflected the night sky. On the ledges above, openmouthed gargoyles leered down at her.

She took a step backward, but retreat was impossible. Daylan slipped a firm arm around her waist as he propelled her forward across the drawbridge. He urged her up some narrow stairs to a huge hall with a ceiling that vaulted two stories high. A crowd of people were milling about waiting to go into the great banquet hall.

Ribbed ceilings, walls decorated with tapestries and medieval decor, which included several armored knights, brought a chill to Maurie that had nothing to do with the lofty hall's slightly dank air. Daylan gave his name to a pretty young woman standing just outside a pair of enormous doors. He was insistent they be seated at a particular table.

''I'm sorry, sir, but those tables are already filled. We can put you on the opposite side.''

"I have reservations," he protested.

"Yes, sir, but fifteen people are seated at each table. We cannot reserve specific seats."

"And why not?"

Though his voice roared in Maurie's ears, she still heard a faint familiar sound coming from the gift shop. On a display table, a gaily painted little horse went round and round to the tinkling tune of "Londonderry Air." Panic rushed through her.

It was happening again!

The melody was a cue for the nightmare. She was in it again. She stood there as rigid as one of the knights in armor.

"Shall we go in, Maurie?"

Maurie. He had called her Maurie. Relief blotted out her bewilderment. She wasn't dreaming.

He took her arm. "Come on, we'd better get seated before they put us in the kitchen," he growled.

His irritation at not getting the seats he wanted barely touched her consciousness. She had a peculiar sensation of being outside herself as she moved beside Daylan into the hall. Long tables filled with diners lined the walls, and at one end of the room stood two thrones on a raised dais. A young bearded king and a pretty blond queen dressed in elegant medieval costumes waved to the crowd of diners as they entered. A huge white dog with a jeweled collar rested at the royal couple's feet, looking bored with the carnival gaiety.

A hostess seated Maurie and Daylan at a far table that gave a poor view of the room and the entertainment. Daylan was not pleased.

"It's all right," she assured him. Two comely maids circled their table with pitchers and laughingly filled tankards with something they called *mede*. It tasted like apple juice to Maurie, but the waitress gave a little spiel about its being a traditional drink made of alcohol fermented with honey and water, with salt, yeast and spices added.

The odd assortment of young and old people at their table showed great enthusiasm for a broth served in small footed bowls that had to be lifted to the mouth for eating. No spoons or forks were allowed. Maurie wondered why they were given knives until wooden trenchers loaded with whole chickens were placed on the table. The people who had been there before grabbed their knives and began hacking pieces off the roasted fowl, putting their booty on the small wooden individual trenchers that served as plates.

"Dig in, dearie," urged a buxom woman on Maurie's left. "Fingers were made before forks," she said, as she grabbed a huge piece of meat in both hands and sank her teeth into it. Grease dripped off her full chin and sprayed the huge homespun bib tied around her fat neck. Eating with one's hands required a good-humored mind-set, decided Maurie.

Despite the hurricane of emotions raging inside her, Maurie tried to get into the mood of the occasion. She

didn't want Daylan to suspect how confused and disoriented she was. She pulled a chunk of bread from a
loaf and managed to nibble on it, as well as a drum-
stick Daylan had put on her plate.

Her stomach was tight and her appetite had fled.
She noticed that Daylan wasn't eating very heartily
himself, and even though he sent her encouraging
grins, the evening was clearly not going to be the suc-
cess he had hoped. He was out of sorts because of the
table they had been given, although Maurie didn't
think it mattered that much. Her nettled thoughts were
centered on the rising fear she'd felt when she had
looked up at the castle and seen the familiar windows
and the gargoyles. She couldn't fight the feeling that
somewhere within the walls of this ancient place was
a bedchamber that matched the one in her dream. Had
it and reality somehow come crashing together?

Food stuck in her cotton-wool mouth, and the meal
seemed to go on for an eternity. She was relieved when
the king, dressed splendidly in tights and a black jeweled tunic complete with a ruche of lace around his
neck, rose to his feet.

"Let the entertainment begin," he said in a loud
pompous voice. He gave a wave of his scepter.

A group of singers dressed in colorful Elizabethan
costumes filed in. The young men and women sang to
the accompaniment of a harp and lute, amid the clang
of tableware as the waitresses moved from the kitchen
to the tables. A juggler entertained the crowd with

balls and flaming swords, and a couple of jesters did a comic routine.

Daylan clapped with the rest, but a hovering shadow in his eyes denied any merriment. When one of the jesters came over to their table, his laughter sounded forced. The buffoon pretended to take a cockroach off Daylan's plate. Everyone around them howled, but Daylan seemed more irritated than amused.

During the meal, Daylan's gaze had roved around the room, making Maurie wonder if he was looking for someone. He obviously had not been pleased with their seats, but was it because their view of the great hall was limited—or something else?

"Will you excuse me, Maurie?" Daylan murmured as he touched her shoulder. He pushed back his chair and was gone before she could even nod.

The hilarity around her echoed in her head like a vibrating drum. Even though she was surrounded by mirth, music and pageantry, she felt strangely removed from it.

The entertainment seemed to go on and on. She looked at her watch. Daylan had been gone nearly fifteen minutes. She glanced around the hall for him, but he was nowhere in sight. Suddenly her attention focused on a young lad dressed in a page uniform who was standing in the arched doorway leading to the outer hall.

Like a flash of videotape, she saw him looking down at her from his bike. The same freckled face, the same mop of curly red hair. She clutched the edge of the table as his words came back to her.

Mrs. Fitzgerald, what are you doing here? Is Miss Doughty with you?

Before she could get to her feet, a blare of trumpets heralded the king and queen's grand march around the room. Maurie was forced to wait in her chair until the royal procession had passed. The parade included knights, ladies-in-waiting, the juggler, jesters and a falconer complete with masked bird on his wrist.

Hurry, Daylan, hurry.

Maurie's heart raced madly as she tried to keep her eyes on the doorway, but her view was blocked as the entourage marched by, banners waving. As soon as the procession passed by her chair, Maurie was on her feet, moving as quickly as she could around the outer edges of the banquet hall. When she reached the doorway, she saw several people standing nearby, but none of them was the redhead.

She frantically moved about the large outer hall, her eyes searching every group that stood laughing and chatting. Lots of young men and women in costume, but no red-haired, freckle-faced lad. Had he been an illusion? A trick of her imagination? She leaned up against one of the cold walls. Her breathing returned to normal and a strange calm came over her.

No, he was real. And someone would know him.

A small sign indicated that the castle office was down the corridor. The office's glass door was closed when she got to it, but there was a bald man standing behind a counter resembling a hotel desk.

Maurie opened the door and went in. She cleared her throat. "Excuse me."

The man looked up, a harried expression on his face. "Yes?"

Maurie moistened her lips. "I wanted to inquire about someone...and I thought you might help me."

"I will if I can," he said with a deep sigh. "I'm just filling in tonight and I'm afraid everything's in a bit of a mess."

"I wanted to ask about a redheaded young man who's wearing a page costume tonight. Could you tell me where I might find him?"

"I haven't the foggiest notion. As I said, I'm just trying to keep things under control tonight. The regular night man had an emergency. I wouldn't know anything about the people working or living here."

"Living here? You mean in the apartments?" She hoped the sudden quiver in her chest didn't show in her voice. "Can you tell me a little bit about them?"

"I'm afraid the suites are all occupied. You'd have to put your name on a waiting list. We only have a few full-time leases, you know."

"I don't want to lease one. I just wanted to inquire about a couple who might be living here." In a calm tone, she inquired about people who had their existence in a nightmare. "Oliver and Dawna Fitzgerald."

He reached for a small ledger. Then his expression eased. "Now I remember the name. I haven't met them, but they have the third-floor suite."

Was he mocking her? Was this whole conversation an insidious twist of her mind? She turned away as a numbness creeping down her spine began to chill her.

"Take the center stairs," he called after her. "Turn to your right at the third-floor landing."

Electric sconces mounted on the thick wall illuminated a steep, narrow stairwell that in medieval days must have smelled of stale air and burning oil. A sense of unreality settled on her but no sense of detachment. Not like her nightmare. She wasn't outside her own body. She was Maurie Miller climbing the stairs of a castle, and with sickening certainty she knew that every step brought her closer to the terror of her nightmare.

When she reached the third-floor landing, she saw a heavily draped window and two ugly leather chairs flanking a three-legged table. There was an elaborately carved door just beyond the furniture and window. Did the rooms in her dream lay beyond its heavy planks? And was the terror she had felt in the throes of her nightmare waiting for her?

Was she about to discover that you could die in a dream?

She walked to the door and raised her hand to knock. Before her knuckles touched the wood, a grip like iron went around her wrist. At the same moment a broad hand muffled her mouth.

"Played me for a fool all the way, didn't you?" He tightened the painful grip on her arm.

She glimpsed his profile, but she couldn't be sure who it was.

Oliver or Daylan?

CHAPTER FIFTEEN

The hall shadows masked his face and his voice was lowered in a hushed growl. "Don't make a sound."

He kept her arm painfully pulled up behind her as he pushed her forward past the main staircase to a small door at the end of the corridor. He shoved her into a room that was scarcely more than a cell. Moonlight slanting through high windows touched piled-up boxes like those in a storeroom.

A bare bulb hung in the center of the room, with a cord dangling from it. As he reached up and pulled it, a radius of light bathed his face. Relief was mixed with utter bewilderment as she stared at him. She wasn't caught in the horrible nightmare—but maybe something worse! "Daylan!"

"Now talk!" he ordered in a impatient tone. "What have you told Fitzgerald?"

"He really exists?" she croaked. The name coming from Daylan's lips was a frightening confirmation.

Daylan gave a short, mirthless laugh. "Lady, you're something else. I suppose you're going to spin that nightmare yarn of yours again."

"It's true, I swear." Her voice quivered. "I know none of it makes sense. But you have to believe me. Oliver Fitzgerald was in my nightmare—just like Miss Doughty and Dr. Ferges."

"You never mentioned him before," he lashed out. "You were very careful not to let on that you knew him."

"I don't know him!"

"But Oliver Fitzgerald is in your dreams?"

"Exactly!"

There was an ugly twist to his mouth. "And you decided not to share this little bit of trivia with me?"

"You would have reacted the same way you did when I told you about the nurse and the doctor. I *know* I've never met them, either. In my nightmare everyone calls me Dawna Fitzgerald. And her husband, Oliver, hates her. Something awful is going to happen to me—I mean, to her."

"And you expect me to believe these ridiculous lies? I have to admit it's the most original cover-up I've ever heard."

"It's the truth. And tonight I saw a boy who called me Mrs. Fitzgerald in a dream—only I don't think I was dreaming."

"Convenient, aren't they? These dreams of yours? You took me in well, but no more. Everything rang clear when I saw you outside Fitzgerald's door."

"I just wanted to see if the rooms were the same as the ones in my dream."

"Stop lying." His voice broke. "I've been praying all along I was wrong."

"About what?"

"I couldn't believe you were playing up to me, spying on my every move. Don't deny it! You played your part very nicely. I was almost taken in. I gambled on my life and the lives of others because I couldn't think straight about my feelings for you. Tonight I waited for you to meet someone or make a move. And you did." His mouth twisted bitterly. "Like a honeybee you flew right into my net."

"What are you talking about?"

"I'm talking about deceit and treachery." He stared at her for a long moment and his voice was raw with emotion as he said, "Like mother, like daughter. 'Tis a betrayal to yourself, Maureen O'Mallory, that you found what you came looking for—yer roots."

The air was thick with distrust and anger during the silent ride back to the boardinghouse. Daylan's profile was chiseled in granite, and Maurie wanted to scream at him, vent her confusion and anxiety. Her nails bit into the flesh of her hands as she gripped them tightly in her lap. How could he turn on her like that? Accusing her of pretending love for him while she wove a web of deceit to ensnare him. The whole thing was preposterous. How could she be in league with someone in a dream? Until tonight she hadn't even known that Oliver Fitzgerald was a real person.

Hot tears welled in her eyes. He thought she'd made up the whole thing. The nightmares. The people in them. A leaden heaviness settled in the pit of her stomach. How could she explain it? She couldn't. There wasn't any logical explanation.

When he stopped the car in front of the farmhouse, she opened her door and got out. He just sat there behind the steering wheel staring ahead. She slammed the door and stalked angrily into the house. After she had shut the front door behind her, she leaned against it for a moment, stilling an urge to rush back out to him. She desperately needed his understanding when her world was spinning like a gyroscope, when her life was without sanity.

Daylan, Daylan. His name caught in her throat as headlights flashed across the front of the house and the car roared away, leaving her in the shadow of the hall. An eternity ago they had stood here, exchanging passionate kisses as rain dripped down their flushed faces.

A feeling of utter desolation mingled with a rise of belligerent stubbornness. Tomorrow she could go back to the castle. She was certain that the answer to the nightmare lay within its thick walls. She firmed her chin and with purposeful steps went upstairs to face a torturous, sleepless night.

The next morning Maurie was in the kitchen early. Once again the landlady seemed surprised to see her there when she came down to fix breakfast. She eyed Maurie's drawn face but didn't say anything.

"Would it be possible for me to borrow the pickup for an errand?" Maurie asked her.

"I reckon so—a bit low on petrol, I'm afraid," the landlady said, the double meaning obvious as she handed her the keys.

"I'll fill the tank," Maurie promised.

Mrs. Duffy lifted an eyebrow. "I didn't see Mr. O'Shane's car this morning. Didn't he bring you home last night?"

Maurie nodded without comment.

The landlady's clear blue eyes measured Maurie's closed expression. "How'd you like the castle and all the folderol?"

"It was . . . quite a show," she said lamely.

Mrs. Duffy offered her a cup of coffee. "Are you two having a spat?"

Maurie responded with a weak smile. "You might say that." *More like a devastating, all-out attack.*

The coastline was partially obscured by early-morning haze as Maurie drove northward in the rickety old truck. Rugged promontories, stark and sheer, fell away to a relentless surf. Had Jake Flintery fallen to his death somewhere along this stretch of cliffs? A cold prickling at the nape of her neck accompanied a mental picture of Maelene O'Mallory fighting with her lover, a fatal slip of footing—and tragedy.

Intentional or accidental? Had Maelene O'Mallory wanted to kill the father of her child?

"Like mother, like daughter." Daylan's accusation roared in her ears. Her hands tightened on the steering wheel. He had condemned her for the blood that ran in her veins.

The large parking area in front of the castle was nearly empty, with only a few cars parked near a side entrance. Maurie brought the truck to a stop, got out and walked to the front of the castle without looking upward as she'd done the night before. She was determined not to give way to any imaginings or fanciful speculation. She would keep her mind centered on the moment and trust her immediate senses.

The front entry hall was deserted and the small gift shop closed. As her footsteps echoed on the wooden floor, the atmosphere was like that of a house after a party, with lingering odors of food, stale cigarette smoke and beer.

Her mind raced ahead of her steps as she climbed the narrow staircase leading to the third floor. What would she do and say when she came face to face with Oliver Fitzgerald or the icy Miss Doughty? Should she ask to see Dawna?

But when I'm Maurie, there is no Dawna.

The constriction in her chest tightened. *And when I'm Dawna, there is no Maurie.*

An icy stab of terror caught at her. *And if Dawna dies, will I be dead, too?*

Her steps faltered. She leaned up against the cold stone wall, trying to control her breathing. The very thing she feared was happening. The edge between her nightmare and reality was blurring. She reined in a panicked urge to turn and flee.

Was she awake or dreaming?

At the top of the stairs, the silhouette of a man looking down at her played in front of her eyes for a brief second and then was gone. Like someone propelled by a force beyond herself, she climbed the remaining steps to the third floor.

Last night, the door to the Fitzgerald apartment had been tightly closed. This morning the door stood open.

An invitation?

A warning?

Maurie moved forward, glancing uneasily about, but she reached the open door without incident. Just inside the apartment was a maid's cart. A young woman in a maid's uniform was piling dirty linen in a laundry bag.

"Oh!" she gasped when she saw Maurie. "I'm sorry, ma'am. I'd have waited to straighten up, but they told me you'd be away for a few days. I saw little Hollie leave with her nanny for the country and I thought you and Mr. Fitzgerald were already gone."

A hopeless despair swept over Maurie. *I'm back in the nightmare again.*

"Did you forget something, Mrs. Fitzgerald?"

Maurie nodded. "Yes, I forgot something." With a jolt, she realized she had spoken in her American accent, not Dawna's crisp British tone.

The maid looked uneasy. "I'm sure a few days' cruising on the water will do you good. I'll just get out of your way." She hastily moved the cart into the hall. As Maurie walked by her, she felt the young woman's eyes raking her from head to toe.

"Wait!" she said as Maurie put her hand on the knob and started to close the door.

Maurie slowly faced her. *She knows something's wrong.* She's going to call someone before she lets me in.

Instead of expressing any doubts, the maid handed her a Don't Disturb sign. "I'm sorry, I accidentally tore the other one," she said.

Maurie thanked her and closed the door. She turned around to face the apartment she had known in her dream. She crossed a small sitting room and stood in a doorway leading into a spacious bedchamber. The wide four-poster bed was there, newly made up with silken covers and pillowcases embroidered with the initials C.C.—Cullen Castle.

Maurie's eyes traveled over the television set, the dressing table and the chaise longue where Hollie and her nanny had sat. For reassurance that she was not caught in the nightmare again, she stood in front of the mirror and stared at her reflection. Short brown hair cupped her cheeks. She was wearing a sweatshirt with the name of her college blazed across it and blue denim jeans.

"I'm Maurie Miller," she said aloud to the room. With slow, deliberate steps, she walked over to the window and fingered the heavy drapery. Looking below she saw an expanse of grass stretching to the edge of the nearby ocean. Slowly she raised her eyes to the same leering gargoyle that had spewed rain out of its mouth. All of it was familiar. She had been here before.

In my nightmare.

How was that possible? How could she dream about this room if she'd never been in it before? Could she have been abducted at some point and brought here in a hypnotic state? Or had the dream been implanted in her mind by some diabolical hypnotist without her knowledge? Even as she grasped at far-out rationalizations, she knew such speculation was nonsense.

No one had abducted her.

Nor hypnotized her.

The images in her dream had come from her subconscious.

She turned away from the window and walked into the spacious bathroom. The fixtures and colored tile were just as she remembered. As she faced the closed door at one side of the room, her pulse quickened, and remembered panic brought a cold moisture to the palms of her hands.

Oliver's room.

She opened the door that connected the bathroom to the adjoining bedroom, half expecting to see Oliver standing there, glaring at her. Even though the room was empty, his voice rang in her ears, lashing out with vicious curses. She began to tremble. Her breathing was shallow and her lips suddenly dry enough to crack.

He's not here, some inner voice assured her.

Her shoes whispered on the thick carpet as she walked over to his desk. The odor of cigarette smoke lingered even though the maid had left a clean ashtray. An expensive desk set lay in an ordered pattern on the newly dusted desk. She opened several empty drawers. Everything appeared as impersonal as most hotel furniture. Her gaze fell to the wastebasket. Empty.

What had she hoped to find? She picked up a folder from the desk in which the management of Cullen Castle listed the services offered. Several colorful photos heralded nearby tourist attractions, including the Cliffs of Moher. Maurie returned the brochure to the desk—and then she saw the edge of a paper sticking out of one of the pages.

She drew it out and saw that it was a scribbled memo of some sort. The maid's comment came back to her. *I'm sure a few days' cruising on the water will do you good.* Was *Blue Neptune* the name of the Fitzgeralds' boat?

She studied the name and dates on the paper. An itinerary of some sort? None of the names were familiar, except one. Danequin? Wasn't that the small harbor that she and Daylan had visited on their trip around the Dingle Peninsula?

Moisture drained out of her mouth. She crumpled the paper in her hand. She had not found the answer to anything—only more questions.

Maurie drove back to Glenmara, drained of energy and emotion. Daylan, Daylan. His name was like a knife in her chest. He had accused her of spying on him. There was only one thing to do—leave Ireland as quickly as possible. She couldn't find her way through the bewildering maze that engulfed her. Truth and fantasy. Where did one end and the other begin? While she still had some control over her mental powers, she had to get back to her life in the States. With luck she could get a flight out later today or in the morning. She would call the airport as soon as she got back to the farmhouse.

She stopped at a station to fill the truck with gas. She was waiting for her change when a strong odor of tansy came through the truck's open window. Tansie's wizened face appeared in the window.

"No." Maurie gripped the steering wheel as dizziness came over her.

Tansie jerked open the door of the pickup. "Bus leaves for Danequin in fifteen minutes." She grabbed Maurie's arm.

"What?" Maurie tried to pull back but found herself outside the truck in spite of her efforts.

Tansie handed her an envelope. "Yer ticket. Be off with ye."

"No, leave me alone."

"Ye must go. Now. There's no time." She pointed to a green bus loading across the street. "The answers you seek are waiting."

The woman's promise was like a light blazing in a tunnel of confusion and despair. "What do you mean?"

Her eyes held Maurie's with a steel-like lock. "You'll find yer way through the dream." Tansie took her hand and pulled her across the street. "'Tis time ye met yerself."

When the bus pulled away Tansie was standing on the sidewalk, a satisfied smile softening her weathered features as she waved goodbye to Maurie, whose peaked face was pressed against the bus window.

CHAPTER SIXTEEN

The motion of the bus and the rhythmic sound of the wheels kept Maurie sitting passively in her seat as the bus headed in a southwesterly direction along the same highway she'd traveled with Daylan. A deep sense of weariness made her lean her head back. She stared at nothing as the bus swayed and the sound of the engine created a steady hum in her ears. Someone coughed in the seat behind her, and a low murmur of voices added to the quiet unreality of the moment.

Imperceptibly, the swaying of the bus changed to a rolling motion. Her eyes closed. She became aware of a rising and falling sensation, instead of a swaying motion. A low hum of an engine mingled with the sound of splashing water.

Tired. So tired.

Awareness came back slowly, crossing her mind like a nebulous shadow until her heavy eyelids lifted. She blinked as a stateroom came into focus. Walls with dark wooden paneling rose to a low ceiling, and polished brass fixtures reflected light from electric sconces mounted on the wall. As she turned her head, curtained portholes met her stunned gaze. She was instantly filled with icy panic.

I'm dreaming again.

She stiffened, fighting the horrible trapped feeling that was more intense than ever before. Panic sprang at her like a saber-toothed tiger. She'd never felt so enclosed. So helpless. As if a net was drawing tighter and tighter around her, she had the terrifying sensation she was being drawn so deeply into the throes of the nightmare that she might never wake up again. A scream caught in her throat.

Was this the way dying people felt, caught between life and death?

She lurched into a sitting position, then tried to stand up, but her legs were like wet pasta. Boat timbers shuddered under her feet as the craft sliced through the water at high speed. She clung to a bunkbed post to keep from falling to the floor. Her stomach lurched with nausea. Her whole body felt disjointed and threatened to float away from her. Her lungs labored for air. She had to get out of the confining cabin. Up on deck where she could breathe.

She lunged toward a leather chair a few feet from the bunk. Grasping the back with both hands, she managed to stay upright. Her shallow gasps of air were short, labored. Her head hung heavy.

Despair washed over her. No matter what she did, she'd still be caught in a torturous dream. It wasn't any use. Why fight a nightmare? She'd never win.

Tears of helplessness spilled down her cheeks. Dreams always thwarted the dreamer.

Dear God, let me wake up.

The only answer to her prayer was the stubbornness that made her reach out for a small stool in front of a built-in bar. She fell on it, managing to keep her rubbery legs under her. Holding on to the edge of the bar, she maintained her balance as she moved along it, gauging the distance that still remained between her and the cabin door.

You can do it.

Taking a deep breath, she staggered across the open space, holding out her hands toward the doorknob. A sudden roll of the boat caught her short of the door and she went down. Arms and legs crumpled under her and she lay on the floor like a rag doll void of stuffing. Tears dribbled down her cheeks and she whimpered like a wounded kitten.

Try again.

The voice was a sharp prod, relentless and unsympathetic. She tried to shut it out and couldn't. With laborious effort, she got to her knees and in a wobbly fashion crawled the remaining few feet to the door. Reaching up, she grabbed the doorknob and pulled herself to her feet again. Her hands were sweaty on the knob. *Please, don't let it be locked.*

Her mouth was dry as she turned the knob. She let out the breath she'd been holding when the door swung open easily. A short, narrow flight of stairs rose to another closed door at the top. A briny smell of sea air filled the passage and touched Maurie's hot cheeks with reassuring briskness.

She reached for a brass railing fastened to the wall and, like a child learning to climb stairs, put both feet on a step before moving up to the next one. There were only six steps, but before she reached the fourth one, the door at the top of the passage opened.

A man stood there, casting a black shadow over her like the spread wings of a vulture.

''Dawna! Get down below.''

He reached for her. With a cry she stepped backward and fell into open air.

Maurie's head came up with a scream lodged in her chest. Where was she? Not in the stateroom. Not on the stairs.

Her eyes fixed on the small window beyond which buildings of a small village flowed by. She bit her trembling lip. She was still on the bus. Everything else was a dream.

The bus turned a corner and came to a stop in front of small pub. ''Twenty minutes,'' announced the driver.

Maurie sat in her seat without moving. The nightmare lingered like the side effects of a drug. Her mouth was dry and her heart thumped loudly like a bass drum gone berserk.

"Come on, miss," urged the driver. "Get yourself a bite of lunch 'fore we're off again."

She managed to get to her feet, but her head was reeling as she followed an exodus of people from the bus and into a small tavern. She managed to drink some black tea and eat a thick slice of bread with yellow cheese even though her stomach remained in a knot. By the time the bus loaded up again, the after-effects had begun to fade.

One thing was certain, she thought as she sat rigidly in her seat, she would not allow herself to doze off again.

The bus rolled on.

People came and went.

As her destination drew nearer, Maurie realized with a sickening twist that she had no idea how to proceed once she reached Danequin. She had no luggage. No place to stay. No idea what she should do.

She stared out the bus window, remembering the way Daylan had treated her when he'd found her outside the Fitzgeralds' suite. He'd assailed her when she tried to tell him the truth. *But what was the truth?*

Hot perspiration beaded on her forehead. She felt out of control. She was being manipulated by forces she couldn't see or understand. Tansie had promised her that she would find the answers she sought. But what if those answers destroyed her?

The bus had stopped at every hamlet along Tralee Bay and the drive around the Dingle Peninsula. Only

four other people were left on the bus when night fell.
When it finally reached Danequin, they got off the bus
along with Maurie and disappeared quickly into the
small town hugging the coastline.

The bus drove off and Maurie stood alone in front
of a small, whitewashed building. The streets were
dimly lighted, and a night mist was already floating in
from the water. What should she do? Where should
she go? She shivered as she started walking along a
boardwalk skirting the edge of the lapping ocean.

She glanced at boats snubbed up to the dock. Most
of them were fishing vessels. When she passed a boat-
house with a sign advertising excursions to the Blasket Islands, she remembered Daylan holding a
conversation in Gaelic with the seaman who owned the
boat. At the time, she had been irritated because she
couldn't understand what they were saying. Now she
knew that he had suspected her of treachery even then.
What had he been talking to the man about? And
those other two disreputable-looking men. What were
they planning? Her lover had glared at her with such
malevolence that it seemed impossible he'd ever held
her passionately in his arms.

She shivered and kept walking down the uneven
wharf. She had almost reached the end of the pier
when her breath caught. Suspended in a pool of haze
like a phantom boat, a modern yacht rocked in the
water just beyond the last arc light. A light shone in

one of the lower portholes, and she could read the name on its hull—*Blue Neptune*.

That's where I was. In her mind's eye she saw clearly the cabin with its dark walls and shiny brass accessories.

As she stood alone at the end of the pier, the scene was as unreal as any in her nightmare. Fog crawled in from the water and gray swirls swept across the dank boards under her feet. A melancholy foghorn sounded somewhere in the distance, above the relentless lapping and sucking of the surf.

Shivering in the dank cold while her forehead glistened with hot sweat, she wanted to be anyplace but here. She was caught helplessly in an existence that was real or imaginary. It didn't matter. If she escaped from one identity, she was only trapped in another. Suddenly a strong wind came rolling down the pier. It was like a hand at her back, urging her forward.

Ye must find yerself.

Maurie moved toward the yacht, which was tugging restlessly at its moorings. No sound came from the craft, and except for that one faint porthole light, it lay in darkness. Deserted. Waiting. Would the horrid nightmare be over if it played itself out?

If Dawna is killed, will I die, too?

Maybe Dawna was already dead. The fall down the stairs could have killed her.

If I look upon her dead face, will I be free?

Once more the night breeze grew stronger, pushing her forward along the side of the yacht until she reached the place where she could slip aboard.

For a long moment she stood on the deck, leaning back against the railing, her senses reaching out like antennae. Then she moved purposefully along the side of the boat. She knew exactly where she'd find the narrow outside door that would lead her down into the dimly lighted stateroom.

And what will I find there?

She swallowed around the knot in her throat as she turned the doorknob.

Locked.

Her trembling fingers moved to the cold metal of the lock. A key was still in it. The lock clicked loudly in her ears as she turned the key, the door swinging open easily under her nervous hand.

Light from the stateroom below spilled up the narrow stairway through the half-open door at the bottom. As Maurie moved slowly down the steps, the brass railing felt familiar under her touch. The terror she'd experienced before on these same steps came back. Her breath caught and for an agonizing moment she thought she was going to faint.

Am I Maurie or Dawna?

CHAPTER SEVENTEEN

With trembling hands Maurie pushed the door all the way open. She stood in the doorway for a long moment and then slowly walked into the stateroom. It was just as she remembered: paneled walls, brass fixtures, a built-in bar and stools, leather chairs and the bunkbed.

I've been here before.

She turned around and saw herself bound to a wooden captain's chair with a gag over her mouth. The woman who *was* and *was not* herself stared at her with pleading eyes.

Maurie stared back, unable to move. The azure blue eyes looking at her were her own. The same shade of dark brown hair framed a face that was a reflection of her own forehead, cheeks and nose.

'Tis time ye met yerself, Tansie had said. But how could this other part of her be flesh and blood? The woman looking at her with frantic eyes was real. Human. Not a subconscious creation. Not a dream.

Whimpering sobs came from the woman's throat. Maurie shook off a paralyzing shock and hurried to her side. This was no nightmare. *I am not the woman bound in the chair.* But the danger was real, and it curled up inside Maurie like a serpent getting ready to strike.

She unknotted the cruel gag over the woman's mouth and untied the cord knotted around her wrists and ankles. Then she said in a hoarse whisper, "Dawna?"

The woman's eyes widened. She raised her hand to touch Maurie's face. "Are you me?"

"I don't think so." Maurie gave her a wry smile. "But I'm not exactly sure. Sometimes I have nightmares about being Dawna Fitzgerald."

Dawna nodded. "And sometimes I feel someone taking over my body," she said in a quivering voice. "Someone stronger than I am. How could that be?"

"I don't know. But there isn't time to sort everything out now. The important thing is that I'm here." Maurie prayed there would be time later to talk about Tansie and her mysterious powers.

"Oliver is going to kill me," Dawna whimpered. "I had to sign the papers. My inheritance. He demanded control of everything. I tried to hold out, but he threatened Hollie. Now he controls everything my parents left me. He doesn't need me alive any longer." Her anguished eyes locked with Maurie's matching ones. "I tried to get away, but I fell on the stairs."

I know. I was there.

"How many people are on the boat?" Maurie asked quickly.

Her lips quivered. "Just three, I think. Oliver and two crewmen. They went ashore a couple of hours ago."

"What about Miss Doughty?"

Dawna shook her head. "No, he left my nurse behind. And sent Hollie to the country with her nanny." Tears welled in her eyes. "I'll never see my little girl again."

"Of course you will!" Maurie answered sharply. "But we've got to get out of here before he comes back." Maurie took her arm. "We have to hurry."

Dawna pulled back from her touch. "No."

"What's the matter?"

"I don't want you to possess me anymore," she said with a sob. "I don't want to give up my mind, my body. Do and say things that aren't me. I'd rather die."

Maurie was too stunned to answer. Dawna's vehemence against the surrender of herself was as strong as her own abhorrence of losing herself in another body. Was death the only escape for both of them? Maybe they would never be free of each other until one of them died. Did a diabolical fate demand that one of them be sacrificed so that the other could live without torment?

I'm the strongest, thought Maurie. I can walk out of here, leave Dawna to the death Oliver has planned for her. Then I'd be free. No more nightmarish out-of-body experiences in Dawna's body, because Dawna would be dead.

Maurie stared at the woman who was a reflection of herself. Even as her mind resisted acceptance, she knew the truth. "We have no choice, Dawna. We'll both survive or we'll die together."

At that moment loud voices on the upper deck told them that the men were back.

"Damn," breathed Maurie.

"What'll we do?" asked Dawna. Fear overtook the resistance she'd shown to Maurie's help a moment ago.

The sound of a key turning in the lock and guttural swearing floated down the stairwell. Maurie had left the key in the unlocked door.

Probably he's confused and is unlocking the door, instead of locking it, thought Maurie.

"When Oliver finds you here, I don't know what he'll do," warned Dawna.

Maurie made the decision in a second. "I'll take your place. Maybe we can fool him long enough for you to get away."

"Why would you do that?" Dawna asked with wonder in her voice. She seemed unable to believe what she was hearing. "I know him. He'll kill you."

Maurie didn't answer. There wasn't time. How could she pass for Dawna in jeans and white sweatshirt with her college's name blazed across it? Dawna was wearing a blue cashmere cardigan and navy slacks.

With a desperate hope that maybe her husband might not notice the change in pants, Maurie stripped off her sweatshirt.

"Give me your sweater." She unbuttoned Dawna's cardigan and stripped it off her arms. Then she thrust her sweatshirt into Dawna's hands.

"Get behind the door. Put this on while Oliver's attention is on me. Sneak up the stairs and off the boat. Can you do it?"

Dawna gave an uncertain nod.

"If you want to see your little girl again, Dawna, find somebody. Anybody. Bring them back."

Maurie gave her an impatient push toward the door and then darted to the captain's chair. She grabbed up the gag, tied it around her mouth and then wrapped a cord around her legs and knotted it clumsily. She put her wrists together in her lap with the cord wrapped loosely around them. Her hair looked about the same length from the front because Dawna's long hair was pinned in a tight roll behind her head.

Maurie sank back in the chair and prayed that she looked the same way Dawna had a few minutes earlier. Fear was like iced water running through her veins. She bit her lip, trying not to tremble. She had seen the cruel hatred in Oliver Fitzgerald's eyes, felt his harsh hand as he struck his wife. By taking Dawna's place, she, Maurie Miller, could be the victim of his murderous intent. If she begged for her life, would he believe that she was someone else? His wife's double?

And if he kills me, will anyone ever know the difference?

Loud footsteps sounded on the stairs. She recognized them as the same threatening footsteps in her dream. Only this time, they were real. And there was no escape.

She knew she had to hold his attention long enough to give Dawna a chance to get away. She hung her head and watched the door out of the corner of her eye.

He came through the entryway, looking exactly the way she had seen him in her nightmares—the same dark eyes and black mustache stretching above a cruel mouth. She had felt the strength of his blows and reeled from his verbal abuse.

As he walked toward her, she tipped over her chair.

"Trying to break your neck to save me the trouble?" he chided with a coarse laugh.

Maurie kept her head lowered and her hands grasped tightly in her lap as she lay in a fetal position on the floor.

"Stupid woman."

She caught a glimpse of the bottom of Dawna's slacks disappearing up the stairway. The woman had been doped and battered until she had little physical or emotional strength left. It would be a miracle if she came through in a life-and-death crisis. Maurie prayed that Dawna had the strength to make it up the stairs and off the boat. Oliver stared down at Maurie, crumpled on the floor, and made no move to touch her.

She waited. *Please, please let him be fooled.*

Without warning, he kicked her in the side with his heavy boot. "You haven't got the sense of a blasted bloody goose, Dawna. Never did."

The pain in Maurie's side was blunted by the victory that he thought she was Dawna. She hunched up as much as she could, trying to stiffen against any more kicks. He thought her weak and helpless from months of sickness brought on by his mental and physical cruelty. In league with the doctor and nurse, Oliver had surely sedated Dawna to the point of illness. Maurie wanted to leap to her feet and battle him with all the fury that surged through her healthy body. But her instinct for self-preservation was strong. It took all the self-control she could muster to meekly accept his abuse.

He swore at her, degrading her beyond belief, and she feared at any moment he would jerk her up and bury his fists in her body. If he looked at her closely, he would know that the ropes were loose around her wrists.

"You could have made it easy on yourself. But no! You had to push me. Torment me. Hold on to every blasted cent until I had no choice. Well, no more!" He swore again in satisfaction. "Now you'll be bait for the fish when we make it out to sea."

He turned his back to her, leaving her on the floor beside the overturned chair. Crossing to a small painting hanging on the wall, he slid the picture to one side, revealing a small safe.

"I'd better put these papers in the safe. Things would have been different if you'd signed them months ago, my stupid little wife. Now there's nothing to be done but make sure you're not around when I start spending your money."

Maurie watched him through half-lowered lids as she lay with her cheek pressed against the floor. His jet black hair and the breadth of his shoulders reminded her of Daylan. She closed her eyes. A sudden fullness brought tears easing down her cheeks. Would Daylan ever know the truth? Why hadn't he believed her? She'd never known Oliver Fitzgerald except in her dreams—until now.

Maurie closed her eyes. *Had Dawna gotten away?* Would she have the strength to find help even if she got away from the boat? She wouldn't be able to walk very far. What if she passed out on the deserted wharf? What if—

Her whirling thoughts jerked to a halt as the floor under her cheek began to vibrate. The rumbling roar of the engine increased in her ears. The boat gave a lurch and started to move.

"Good," growled Oliver with satisfaction. "We're under way."

Panic caught in her chest. *They were putting out to sea. No help was coming.*

His laugh was coarse. "How about a little midnight swim, wifie?"

He disappeared up the stairs, and Maurie heard a loud exchange of men's voices but couldn't make out the words. She threw off the gag and cords and ran to the porthole. Jerking back the curtain, she pressed her face against the glass. Dotted lights and the dark line of land were fast disappearing. Even if she dashed up on deck and jumped overboard, the distance was already too great. She'd never be able to swim back to shore. She was trapped on the boat as Dawna Fitzgerald. Oliver would never believe he had the wrong woman. Would he?

For a desperate moment she grasped at a tenuous hope. He wouldn't kill the wrong woman, would he? All she had to do was convince him she wasn't Dawna and then . . . *And then he'll kill me, anyway.*

CHAPTER EIGHTEEN

Maurie searched the stateroom for any kind of weapon. No luck. Oliver might have anticipated his wife doing the same thing, because the cabin didn't offer so much as a letter opener. All built-in cabinets were locked. Bookcases were filled with nothing but books. Even the liquor cabinet was locked. A small closet contained nothing but a few of Dawna's clothes. Maurie couldn't find anything that might serve as a club or knife. The walls of the stateroom crowded in on her like a cage holding her prisoner until Oliver was ready to drag her up on deck.

What should she do? In answer, a cool draft hit her legs. Fresh air. She spun around and opened the cabin door that Oliver had shut. She peered up the narrow stairway. The upper door was slightly ajar as if in his haste he'd neglected to shut it tightly.

That means it isn't locked.

Maurie didn't move. Maybe he had left it open on purpose. But Oliver didn't know she was free of her bonds. *Or did he?* Was he playing some kind of game? He might be tormenting his wife, making her think she had a chance of escape, but once she was up on deck . . .

Her thoughts reeled in every direction, but one thing was certain. She was helpless if she stayed below. She could hear water sluicing away from the hull and the roar of the engine. The boat rolled to one side as if making a sharp turn. How far out to sea were they going? How soon would Oliver be coming down for her? *Or was he waiting for her to come up on deck?*

If Oliver didn't know she was free of her bonds, there was a chance she might be able to find some kind of weapon on deck to defend herself. The brutal kick he had landed on her when she lay helplessly at his feet had left her side sore and bruised. She wouldn't hesitate to return the blow if the opportunity presented itself.

She started up the stairs. Anything was better than waiting below, she told herself while another inner voice chided her for a fool. What chance did she have against three strong men who could toss her overboard?

Her pulse was pounding loudly when she reached the top step. With her breath a hard lump in her chest, she eased open the door and slipped out onto the deck. The boat was bathed in the darkness of sky and sea as it moved at a high speed through the water.

Pressing up against the side of the boat, she tried to get her bearings. Wind whipped her face and hair, water droplets sprayed over the deck, bathing her in a light mist and blurring her vision. Light poured out on the water from the bow of the boat as it raced forward.

She peered through the darkness. Sparse lights flickered on the horizon. A dark mound in the sea hinted of land. Her heart leapt. An island? Her mind raced ahead. If the boat docked, she could vault over the side and run to safety before Oliver even knew she was gone. Energy surged through her. Every muscle was tensed as she waited for the lights to get closer.

Every second was an eternity. While they were still a good distance from the land, the boat slowed down. Maurie's heart plunged. The roar of the engine died away and the yacht bobbed in the water before she heard the anchor slide out of its casing into the depths.

The hope born a moment earlier died. The boat wasn't going to tie up at any wharf. She was trapped on board without any possibility of escaping.

She was debating what she should do when two men came out on deck and stood at the stern, looking back at something in the watery darkness. She didn't see the other craft until it slid like a dark whale close to the yacht. In the next minute, ropes had snubbed the two boats together.

Muffled voices and shuffling feet broke the silence as men poured over the stern of the yacht a few feet from where she pressed against the side. Like a small legion of ants they began carrying cargo from the yacht to the waiting gray boat.

"Watch it!"

"Drop that crate and we'll all go up in pieces."

"How many more?"

"Ought to do the job for Queen and country," said a sneering voice.

"Good job, Fitzgerald. We'll see that everything finds it way north."

"Cast off the ropes."

"When do you expect to buy the next shipment of contraband, Fitzgerald?" called someone from the deck of the smaller boat.

Maurie couldn't hear Oliver's answer because at that moment a man came along the deck and was upon her before she could dash back down the stairs.

"What in hell?" he swore as he saw her. "Oliver," he yelled as he made a grab for her.

Maurie evaded his grasp and ran the only way she could—toward the stern of the boat. Oliver swung around at the sound of his name. When he saw her, his expression was one of satanical fury.

She couldn't go forward without putting herself in his clutches. The man behind her cut off any retreat. At that moment, the other boat slid by the side of the *Blue Neptune* with only about a yard between the two crafts. In desperation Maurie gave a flying leap over the railing and fell down on the deck of the other boat as it slowly moved past the yacht.

Before Oliver could register what had happened, the distance between the two boats was too wide to jump.

He stood at the railing, waving his arms and shouting, "Bring the boat back. Now!"

Two pairs of rough hands pulled Maurie to her feet.

"Don't let her go!" ordered Oliver. "Come back!"

In response, the boat turned sharply around in a tight circle.

"Watch it!" someone cried. But the warning came too late. The heavy cargo that had been hastily loaded on the deck shifted, and the weight suddenly plunging to one side of the boat was too much, too fast.

In slow motion, the boat began to roll. Water poured onto the deck. Maurie screamed as she was flung overboard.

She was drawn down into the swirling black depths of the cold waters of the Atlantic. She flung out her arms and legs, holding her breath as she pumped upward. Her lungs were bursting when she broke through the surface after a terrifying eternity in the black water. She gasped air as she struggled to remain on the surface. All around her boxes and crates were sinking from sight. A bright light from the yacht played over the water as the men who'd gone overboard with her climbed up its side.

She tread water. Even as her strength ebbed and she knew she couldn't stay afloat for more than a few more minutes, she couldn't put herself back in Oliver's clutches.

Maybe I'm dreaming.

Would she wake up safe? Was death by drowning just a figment of her subconscious? Or had the nightmare become real? She saw Oliver's black head just a few feet away. *He's jumped in after me.* Awake or dreaming, he was going to see to it that she would die.

She struck out in the water, desperately trying to get away, but he was upon her before she had taken a dozen strokes. His fist lashed out and caught her chin in a direct blow. Pain exploded in a thousand colors behind her eyes, shattering the image of his face into a thousand pieces.

Her chest was on fire and bitter bile surged into her mouth. She turned her head to the side. No longer in the water, she could feel the rolling motion of the boat under her. Firm hands turned her over. Her eyes fixed on the face above her and a cry caught in her throat. Not Oliver. Daylan!

At that moment an orange fireball leapt into the air, and pieces of wood and debris rained down upon them. Daylan threw himself over her. Smothered against his wet chest, she could hardly breathe. Even as she struggled, he kept her firmly in the shelter of his body. She heard men running and guns firing.

Shouting.

Another explosion.

He jerked to his feet, lifted her up in his arms and carried her into a small cabin. Wet clothes were plastered against his body, and his dark hair fell in a wet cap around his face. He put her down on a leather couch. His expression was grim, and she remembered that he had struck her with a hard fist in the water.

He took two blankets from an overhead cupboard. "Here. Strip out of those wet clothes."

She tried to do as he ordered, but her fingers were cold and numb and wouldn't work the buttons on Dawna's cardigan. He brushed her hands aside and began to undress her. Keeping his eyes away from her face and moving with impersonal efficiency, he removed the clothes from her shivering body.

She remembered how he had undressed her with tantalizing loving care during that weekend, kissing and caressing her as each garment fell to the floor. None of that tenderness was evident in his touch now, as he wrapped the blankets around her nakedness.

Then he pulled out a duffel bag full of clothes and, with his back to her, stripped out of his own wet garments. She knew every ripple in his muscular back and her eyes followed the firmness of his thighs and legs. The passionate joy in his arms might never have been. Only contempt was in his eyes now when he looked at her. Her sluggish mind struggled to find some thread of coherent thought.

"Where did this boat come from?" she asked him.

"The Basket Islands. It's a government patrol boat," Daylan answered curtly. "We knew the Fitzgerald yacht was scheduled to rendezvous in these waters. And we were waiting."

"Thank God," she breathed.

"Cut out the playacting, Maurie," he ordered angrily. "You were in on the whole miserable business. You made haste to Danequin in order to be in on the delivery of arms to the smugglers. Was it only last night that you were swearing with tearful eyes that you didn't even know Oliver Fitzgerald?" he asked with a mocking sneer.

"I was telling the truth."

"Don't play me for an idiot, Maurie. I watched the well-planned transfer of contraband and I saw you playing the foolhardy show-off. Too bad you got more excitement than you bargained for when the cargo shifted."

"I was trying to get away. Oliver was going to kill me." Her voice cracked with anger. How could he be so blind as to think she made that dangerous jump just for sport? "If you think I'm one of Oliver's accomplices, why did you jump in the water to save me?"

"Why, indeed?" he echoed as if he'd been avoiding the same question.

Fury over his stubborn blindness made her lash out. "You lied to me from the very beginning. All that garbage about meeting with those men on business. Why didn't you tell me the truth?"

"I couldn't. You presented a risk, and I couldn't gamble with our informers' lives."

"So much of a risk that you had to play me for a lovesick fool," she countered bitterly.

"I wanted to be wrong about you. Lord, how I wanted to be wrong. My feelings for you have been tearing me apart. I'm with MI5—British Intelligence. I'm on assignment with the Irish authorities to try to stop the flow of illegal arms to terrorists responsible for attacks on mainland Britain."

Her love was so desperate, so all-consuming, that she was reduced to an emotional beggar. "I love you. Please, please believe me."

"God knows I wish I could," he responded in the same kind of tortured voice. "But the facts speak for themselves. I left you at the farmhouse last night. And here you are twenty-four hours later on a boat with Oliver Fitzgerald as he makes an illegal delivery of arms to known terrorists. A coincidence that would stretch the faith of even the most hopeless lover."

"Then you do love me," she said, a spurt of hope washing away the harshness of his words.

"My feelings are of no consequence." His eyes were as hard as flint, his tone brittle. "My job is to bring to justice anyone guilty of aiding and abetting terrorists, who maim young children and murder innocent people. I didn't want to believe you were connected with Fitzgerald and his secret Avengers."

"I'm not! I didn't know anything about him. I never met him until tonight except . . . except . . ."

"I know. Except in your dream," he scoffed. "I suppose you had a dream that told you to come to Danequin and get aboard his yacht."

"Not a dream. Tansie."

"Tansie!" His short laugh was mocking. "So it's Tansie, is it? And why did she tell you to leave Glenmara to join Fitzgerald?"

'Tis time ye met yerself. Maurie swallowed back the words.

"Well?" Daylan prodded impatiently.

"I look like Dawna Fitzgerald, and in my nightmares I become her." Maurie bit her lip and then stuck out her chin. "Tansie knew Dawna was in trouble, and I believe she sent me to Danequin so I could help. When I got to the *Blue Neptune,* Dawna was tied up. Oliver was going to kill her now that she'd signed the papers giving him control of her money."

She kept her eyes away from Daylan's face as she talked, but she could feel angry disbelief radiating from him. "I took Dawna's place and fooled Oliver into thinking I was his wife." Her voice faltered. "I hope she made it off the boat. I don't know for sure."

"Let me get this straight. You rescued Mrs. Fitzgerald from her husband?"

"It's the truth. I can show you the stateroom, the gag, the ropes. You'll have to believe me when you see the evidence with your own eyes."

"I'm afraid that won't be possible." He yanked back a curtain and gave a short jerk of his head. Some distance away, the yacht and smugglers' boat were sending jagged flames into the sky as they slowly sank beneath the black waters of the ocean.

What if Dawna hadn't gotten off the boat?

Maurie's chest tightened painfully. The man who had caught her earlier on the yacht looked astounded—as if he already had one Mrs. Fitzgerald in hand somewhere else. Maybe Dawna had been discovered before she could get off the yacht.

"Where is Oliver?" Maurie asked in a leaden tone.

"Does it matter?" he asked with a cruel twist to his lips. "You'll always have him in your dreams."

Her eyes rounded in horror. An anguished cry broke from her throat. Was she trapped forever in the torturing nightmares? No! She couldn't take any more. She gave into a spasm of weeping that shook her whole body.

Daylan's arms went around her. He was instantly contrite. "I'm sorry, *leannan*. Forgive me. Oliver Fitzgerald didn't make if off the boat. You were the last one brought from the water."

Maurie sobbed in relief. "I don't understand any of this, but I'm telling you the truth." She searched his eyes and saw an anxious sincerity reflected in their depths. Encouraged, she moistened her dry lips. "The first time I had the nightmare I dreamed I was in the Fitzgeralds' apartment at Cullen Castle. I went there this morning, and everything in my dream was the way it really is."

Was it only this morning? Not a lifetime ago?

"Go on," he urged softly but firmly.

"Somehow in my nightmares, I became Dawna Fitzgerald, Hollie's mother and Oliver's wife. No one but little Hollie seemed to know I wasn't Dawna." Maurie stopped for a moment and then told Daylan about Dawna's anxiety about someone else possessing her body.

"But if it was only a dream . . ." protested Daylan.

"I thought I was dreaming everything, but I guess I wasn't. The people in my nightmares were a part of Dawna's existence, but sometimes I met them when I was myself. That's what was so confusing. I didn't know whether I was in my own body or hers. Don't ask me how it happened, but somehow there was a body transference. I left mine and entered Dawna's."

"But how . . . how could you become someone else? Come on, now. Surely you don't believe that kind of thing can happen?"

"I *know* what happened to me."

She saw the struggle going on in his mind. When he didn't answer, she said firmly, "I think Tansie had something to do with it. Everyone says she was dismissed from the Catholic order because of bizarre, unexplained happenings. There are stories about how she cast spells to make people do things. I'm positive she uses tansy flowers to work her magical powers."

He brushed a hand through his damp hair. "All right, given that your nightmares are not dreams, how do you explain transferring into someone who looks like you?"

She frowned. "I don't know. Unless . . ." Her voice trailed off.

"Unless Maelene O'Mallory gave birth to twins," he finished.

"If I have a twin sister, Tansie would know it. She was there."

"It could have happened that there were two babies, I suppose," said Daylan begrudgingly. "You could have been adopted by American parents and Dawna by another. That would explain why the two of you look so much alike."

"When I came back to Ireland to find my roots," reasoned Maurie, "Tansie could have used her witchcraft powers to bring us together."

He gently touched the tears rolling down her cheeks. "What you're saying is beyond my comprehension, *leannan,* I don't understand any of it. Maybe doubts and suspicions have closed my mind. Please, tell me everything from the beginning," he said, his voice softening.

She moistened her lips, trying to put into perspective this new possible revelation that she and Dawna were identical twins.

A knock sounded on the door.

"Yes?" Daylan answered briskly.

A young seaman stuck his head in. "Sorry, sir, but a message has just come through for you. A hospital on the peninsula reports they have just admitted a Dawna Fitzgerald."

Joy and relief surged through Maurie. Dawna was safe.

"The lady is hysterical about someone being held prisoner on her husband's boat." The seaman added, "A young woman who looks like herself."

"Send a message that the young woman is safe," Daylan told him.

"Yes, sir."

The door closed and Daylan tightened the arm he had around Maurie's shoulder. "So it's true." His expression revealed the struggle he was having accepting the unbelievable. "I knew that Fitzgerald had a wife, but I'd never met her. She was reported to be a recluse."

"I think that somehow the past and the present are tangled together," she offered. "When we talk to Dawna, maybe we'll be able to understand how they are connected."

He nodded and his expression became infinitely tender. "Well, I surrender to the one truth that can no longer be denied."

Her mouth parted in a soft smile. She waited to hear the words that echoed in her own heart.

"I love you, Maureen O'Mallory Miller."

Happiness brought a luminous joy to her face. Everything could be set aside except the feelings they had for each other.

"Sure and I love ye, too, Daylan O'Shane," she said, imitating his brogue. "'Tis mine ye'll be, now and forever."

She raised her lips to his as if she dared any fate to declare otherwise.

CHAPTER NINETEEN

When Maurie and Daylan visited Dawna in the small convent hospital, they found her sitting in a sunny room, looking out the window at the rolling sea. When she heard their footsteps, she turned around and a tentative smile crossed her face. "It's over, isn't it?"

Maurie nodded, reached out her arms and hugged the likeness of herself.

Daylan looked from one face to the other—the same deep brown hair, azure blue eyes and bone structure. "It's unbelievable."

Maurie laughed. "Yes, isn't it?"

"I've been expecting you," said Dawna, as she held out a sprig of pale green needlelike leaves to Maurie. "One of my visitors left it for you. Rosemary for remembrance, she said."

"Tansie." Maurie exchanged a knowing look with Daylan.

"She didn't tell me her name," Dawna said with a slight frown. "But she wore a nun's habit and stood by my bedside at dawn. At first I thought I was dreaming, but her voice was clear and compelling. I asked the Mother Superior about her later, but she said there wasn't any nun like the one I had described. Peculiar, isn't it?"

Daylan sighed in resignation. "I'll have to concede that all of this goes beyond my comprehension. Impossible as it may be, there seems little doubt that Tansie was the catalyst that brought you two together."

"She told me she was the nurse in attendance when my mother, Maelene O'Mallory, gave birth to twin girls." Dawna smiled at Maurie. "You and me."

"And did she tell you about our father?" Maurie asked with a raw edge to her voice.

"Yes. Harold Halstead, a young Englishman."

"Who?" gasped Maurie.

Dawna nodded. "He was a student at Oxford University and was in the area doing research on a thesis."

"But Jake Flintery was believed to be Maelene O'Mallory's lover."

Dawna shook her head. "Flintery saw her and wanted her, the woman told me, but she was already in love with Halstead. The two men fought over her, and in the struggle the rebel leader fell to his death. A few days later, Halstead, our father, was shot by a member of the Avengers."

Daylan reasoned, "Then Maelene was already pregnant when Halstead was killed. She went to the home, and when she died, both of you were put up for

adoption. Maurie was taken to America and you...?"
He looked quizzically at Dawna.

"England. My adoptive parents belonged to a ti-
tled family, and I was raised in wonderful circumstances. When they died, I inherited everything." Her
lips quivered. "I married Oliver and learned too late
that he was involved in the Irish struggle. He was determined to get control of my money.... Well, you
know the rest."

Maurie took Dawna's hands in her own. "Whatever strange forces have brought us together, it can
only be a blessing for both of us. I know our mother
would be very happy to know we've found each
other."

The spill gate of Maurie's emotions had been flung
open wide. Last night, Daylan had fulfilled every
dream of happiness as they lay in each other's arms
and looked to the future. They made plans to be married in the same little church that her mother had at-
tended. Maurie would be of his faith and claim the
country of her birth for their children.

"I'm wondering," Daylan said thoughtfully as he
looked at the two glowing young women. "Perhaps we
can locate some of your paternal relatives now that we
know the name of your father. I suspect the Halstead
family will be delighted with the addition of two
beautiful members to their family."

Maurie turned shining eyes on him. "I can't believe it. In my search for my roots, I've not only found

the man I love with all my heart, but a wonderful sister, a beautiful little niece, and now I may even find my grandparents.''

Daylan bent his head to hers and brushed a kiss across her lips. ''It's just as I promised, my precious *leannan,*'' he whispered. ''After the rain...a rainbow.''

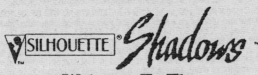

SILHOUETTE® Shadows™

Welcome To The Dark Side Of Love...

AVAILABLE THIS MONTH

#15 FOOTSTEPS IN THE NIGHT—Lee Karr
Anxious to learn about her true family heritage, Maurie Miller traveled to Ireland, only to land in a nightmare. Someone had mistaken her for another woman—a woman who shared the same face—a woman in grave danger.... Maurie had but one chance of survival—Daylan O'Shane, the handsome neighbor who watched her every move.

#16 WHAT WAITS BELOW—Jane Toombs
When Kendra Tremaine inherited her family's estate, she also inherited the menacing legend of Lynx Lake. People had ended up missing or dead at the hands of a mysterious entity, and Kendra wanted some answers. Would she find an ally in Hart Rainwalker, the enigmatic groundskeeper who harbored a secret agenda as well as a blatant attraction?

COMING NEXT MONTH

#17 THE HAUNTING OF BRIER ROSE—Patricia Simpson
With her twenty-first birthday quickly approaching, Rose Quennel vowed to break the chain of dark possession that had cursed both her mother and grandmother. But a midnight shadow threatened to fulfill the legacy by arousing forbidden desires. Could mysterious Taylor Wolfe help end the nightmares, or was he responsible for the midnight madness?

#18 TWILIGHT PHANTASIES—Maggie Shayne
Tamara Dey never knew about her connection to the undead; her guardian kept it a secret to advance his research. Now Eric Marquand appeared in Tamara's life, inspiring an irresistible attraction and haunting feelings of remembrance. But could their love transcend the curse of immortality?

OFFICIAL RULES • MILLION DOLLAR SWEEPSTAKES
NO PURCHASE OR OBLIGATION NECESSARY TO ENTER

To enter, follow the directions published. **ALTERNATE MEANS OF ENTRY:** Hand print your name and address on a 3"x5" card and mail to either: Silhouette "Match 3," 3010 Walden Ave., P.O. Box 1867, Buffalo, NY 14269-1867, or Silhouette "Match 3," P.O. Box 609, Fort Erie, Ontario L2A 5X3, and we will assign your Sweepstakes numbers. (Limit: one entry per envelope.) For eligibility, entries must be received no later than March 31, 1994. No responsibility is assumed for lost, late or misdirected entries.

Upon receipt of entry, Sweepstakes numbers will be assigned. To determine winners, Sweepstakes numbers will be compared against a list of randomly preselected prizewinning numbers. In the event all prizes are not claimed via the return of prizewinning numbers, random drawings will be held from among all other entries received to award unclaimed prizes.

Prizewinners will be determined no later than May 30, 1994. Selection of winning numbers and random drawings are under the supervision of D.L. Blair, Inc., an independent judging organization, whose decisions are final. One prize to a family or organization. No substitution will be made for any prize, except as offered. Taxes and duties on all prizes are the sole responsibility of winners. Winners will be notified by mail. Chances of winning are determined by the number of entries distributed and received.

Sweepstakes open to persons 18 years of age or older, except employees and immediate family members of Torstar Corporation, D.L. Blair, Inc., their affiliates, subsidiaries and all other agencies, entities and persons connected with the use, marketing or conduct of this Sweepstakes. All applicable laws and regulations apply. Sweepstakes offer void wherever prohibited by law. Any litigation within the province of Quebec respecting the conduct and awarding of a prize in this Sweepstakes must be submitted to the Régies des Loteries et Courses du Quebec. In order to win a prize, residents of Canada will be required to correctly answer a time-limited arithmetical skill-testing question. Values of all prizes are in U.S. currency.

Winners of major prizes will be obligated to sign and return an affidavit of eligibility and release of liability within 30 days of notification. In the event of non-compliance within this time period, prize may be awarded to an alternate winner. Any prize or prize notification returned as undeliverable will result in the awarding of that prize to an alternate winner. By acceptance of their prize, winners consent to use of their names, photographs or other likenesses for purposes of advertising, trade and promotion on behalf of Torstar Corporation without further compensation, unless prohibited by law.

This Sweepstakes is presented by Torstar Corporation, its subsidiaries and affiliates in conjunction with book, merchandise and/or product offerings. Prizes are as follows: Grand Prize–$1,000,000 (payable at $33,333.33 a year for 30 years). First through Sixth Prizes may be presented in different creative executions, each with the following approximate values: First Prize–$35,000; Second Prize–$10,000; 2 Third Prizes–$5,000 each; 5 Fourth Prizes–$1,000 each; 10 Fifth Prizes–$250 each; 1,000 Sixth Prizes–$100 each. Prizewinners will have the opportunity of selecting any prize offered for that level. A travel-prize option, if offered and selected by winner, must be completed within 12 months of selection and is subject to hotel and flight accommodations availability. Torstar Corporation may present this Sweepstakes utilizing names other than Million Dollar Sweepstakes. For a current list of all prize options offered within prize levels and all names the Sweepstakes may utilize, send a self-addressed, stamped envelope (WA residents need not affix return postage) to: Million Dollar Sweepstakes Prize Options/Names, P.O. Box 4710, Blair, NE 68009.

The Extra Bonus Prize will be awarded in a random drawing to be conducted no later than May 30, 1994 from among all entries received. To qualify, entries must be received by March 31, 1994 and comply with published directions. No purchase necessary. For complete rules, send a self-addressed, stamped envelope (WA residents need not affix return postage) to: Extra Bonus Prize Rules, P.O. Box 4600, Blair, NE 68009.

For a list of prizewinners (available after July 31, 1994) send a separate, stamped, self-addressed envelope to: Million Dollar Sweepstakes Winners, P.O. Box 4728, Blair, NE 68009.

SWP-09/93

Silhouette Books
is proud to present
our best authors,
their best books...
and the best in
your reading pleasure!

Throughout 1993, look for exciting
books by these top names in
contemporary romance:

DIANA PALMER—
Fire and Ice in June

ELIZABETH LOWELL—
Fever in July

CATHERINE COULTER—
Afterglow in August

LINDA HOWARD—
Come Lie With Me in September

When it comes to passion,
we wrote the book.

BOBT2

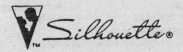

MEN MADE IN AMERICA

Fifty red-blooded, white-hot, true-blue hunks from every State in the Union!

Beginning in May, look for MEN MADE IN AMERICA! Written by some of our most popular authors, these stories feature fifty of the strongest, sexiest men, each from a different state in the union!

Two titles available every other month at your favorite retail outlet.

In September, look for:

DECEPTIONS by Annette Broadrick (California)
STORMWALKER by Dallas Schulze (Colorado)

In November, look for:

STRAIGHT FROM THE HEART by Barbara Delinsky (Connecticut)
AUTHOR'S CHOICE by Elizabeth August (Delaware)

You won't be able to resist MEN MADE IN AMERICA!

If you missed your state or would like to order any other states that have already been published, send your name, address, zip or postal code, along with a check or money order (please do not send cash) for $3.59 for each book, plus 75¢ postage and handling ($1.00 in Canada), payable to Harlequin Reader Service, to:

In the U.S.
3010 Walden Avenue
P.O. Box 1369
Buffalo, NY 14269-1369

In Canada
P.O. Box 609
Fort Erie, Ontario
L2A 5X3

Please specify book title(s) with order.
Canadian residents add applicable federal and provincial taxes.

MEN993

And now for something completely different from Silhouette....

SPELLBOUND
R O M A N C E

Every once in a while, Silhouette brings you a book that is truly unique and innovative, taking you into the world of paranormal happenings. And now these stories will carry our special "Spellbound" flash, letting you know that you're in for a truly exciting reading experience!

In October, look for *McLain's Law* (IM #528) by Kylie Brant

Lieutenant Detective Connor McLain believes only in what he can see—until Michele Easton's haunting visions help him solve a case...and her love opens his heart!

McLain's Law is also the Intimate Moments "Premiere" title, introducing you to a debut author, sure to be the star of tomorrow!

Available in October...only from Silhouette Intimate Moments

SPELL1

NORA ROBERTS

Love has a language all its own, and for centuries flowers have symbolized love's finest expression. Discover the language of flowers—and love—in this romantic collection of 48 favorite books by bestselling author Nora Roberts.

Two titles are available every other month at your favorite retail outlet.

In October, look for:

Affaire Royale, Volume #35
Less of a Stranger, Volume #36

In December, look for:

Command Performance, Volume #37
Blithe Images, Volume #38

Collect all 48 titles
and become fluent in

THE LANGUAGE of LOVE

Silhouette®

If you missed any of volumes 1 through 34, order now by sending your name, address, zip or postal code, along with a check or money order (please do not send cash) for $3.59 for each volume, plus 75¢ postage and handling ($1.00 in Canada), payable to Silhouette Books, to:

In the U.S.
3010 Walden Avenue
P.O. Box 1396
Buffalo, NY 14269-1396

In Canada
P.O. Box 609
Fort Erie, Ontario
L2A 5X3

Please specify book title(s) with order.
Canadian residents add applicable federal and provincial taxes.

LOL1093

HE'S AN

AMERICAN HERO

He's a cop, a fire fighter or even just a fearless drifter who gets the job done when ordinary men have given up. And you'll find one American Hero every month, only in Intimate Moments— created by some of your favorite authors. Look at what we've lined up for the last months of 1993:

October: GABLE'S LADY by Linda Turner—With a ranch to save and a teenage sister to protect, Gable Rawlings already has a handful of trouble...until hotheaded Josey O'Brian makes it an armful....

November: NIGHTSHADE by Nora Roberts—Murder and a runaway's disappearance force Colt Nightshade and Lt. Althea Grayson into an uneasy alliance....

December: LOST WARRIORS by Rachel Lee—With one war behind him, Medevac pilot Billy Joe Yuma still has the strength to fight off the affections of the one woman he can never have....

AMERICAN HEROES: Men who give all they've got for their country, their work—the women they love.

IMHER06

INTIMATE MOMENTS® Silhouette®

Next month, don't miss meeting the Rawlings family of New Mexico. You'll learn to love them!

Look for

Linda Turner's exciting new miniseries.

Look for GABLE'S LADY (IM #523), October's American Hero title.

And look for his siblings' stories as the exciting saga continues throughout 1994! Only from Silhouette Intimate Moments.

WILD-G